ROUGH LOVE

SCREAMING DEMONS MC
BOOK NINE

SUMMER COOPER
SIENNA CHANCE

LOVY BOOKS

Mia tried to think of anyone Sage could've mentioned by the name Laura but she couldn't remember anything. He hadn't shared much of his past with her yet and she was sure that he wouldn't but now he would have to. She was 100 percent sure he had never mentioned her before and so the whole situation didn't make sense to her. She knew the only person who could answer her questions was Sage and she decided to call him immediately. He was the only person who could clear all the mess up.

There was no way for her to handle the situation on her own. She had no idea who the woman was nor did she know who Laura was and what she meant to Sage. It was hard for her to think that he had someone else. It was almost impossible for him to be with her and someone else at the same time but Mia knew that some men were capable of that, capable of cheating on women they claimed to care about. Could that be what was going on? Had Sage already gotten bored of her? A part of her thought that is was unlikely, especially after the step he had taken with her. It wouldn't make sense for him to all of a sudden be seeing someone else too. Mia tried not to think about it. She didn't want to think of Sage with someone else.

Of course, Mia knew that he had been with other women in the past. After all, he was 29 and wildly gorgeous but this woman was claiming that she was going to take him back. That was the one thing that didn't sit right with her. Although Sage wasn't an object anyone could claim, the thought of him possibly seeing her and leaving with her made a lump form in Mia's throat. It was possible that he just hadn't recognized her the first time which was why he didn't do anything but even that confused Mia since he had seen the woman's face. Had he just pretended not to know her, she wondered.

Pulling out her phone, Mia dialed Sage's number. After a few rings, he picked up.

"Mia, is everything okay?" he asked. She could hear the concern in his voice. He sounded so genuine it didn't feel like he could have someone else in his life besides Mia.

She took a deep breath and knew that she wasn't

going to sugarcoat the situation. She wanted him to react so she could gage where she stood.

"Laura is here," she replied.

Sage didn't reply immediately and a sinking feeling filled Mia's chest. She knew that he recognized the name and she didn't need to see his face to know that. His hesitation told her everything she needed to know.

"Did you say Laura?" he asked. His voice sounded shaky and shocked. Mia knew the name meant something but he hadn't mentioned it to her before.

"Yes, you heard correctly, Laura. I think you need to get here right now and explain exactly what's going on," Mia said angrily. She couldn't help it. She didn't know how to contain the feelings she had in her chest, she just didn't know how to handle the situation.

"Laura? But that's not possible…" he replied.

"Either way you need to get here, Sage," Mia said, her patience for the situation running thin. She watched Lorraine from the corner of her eye, sat hunched over the bar, her head in her hands while her sobbing continued to echo around her.

"Okay, I'll be there as quickly as I possibly can," he replied. His voice sounded worried, and the feeling in Mia's chest got worse.

The whole situation still didn't make any sense to Mia as her mind kept going back to the first night she and Sage had met Lorraine, now Laura. He didn't act as if he knew her at all and he had seen her. How could he have seen someone he supposedly loved and not recognized her? Mia knew Laura said she doesn't look the same now but how much can a person really change, and why would they change as well? None of it sat right with Mia the longer she thought about it.

She felt like she wanted to just run away, run away from the mess and drama that had been happening recently. It was all becoming too much for her to handle. It was as if no matter where she went, drama followed close behind her, threatening to ruin her life. She thought about the bad karma that she could possibly have hanging over her. Maybe because she had disappointed her family and done so many bad things growing up, she was getting punished. Could it be that whenever she got comfortable with life something would shift and just fuck it all up for her? She thought that it might be a good explanation for everything.

Mia couldn't stand still as she waited for Sage to show up. She took to pacing the floor by the bar as she waited, her heartbeat racing in her chest as the anticipation built. If Sage left her now, she would be completely heartbroken. They had grown so much recently that thinking of them separating killed her but she had to look at it from all sides. She wasn't sure how long Sage and Laura had been together before he had met Mia but she knew she couldn't be the person that stood between true love and its happy ending, even if it felt like someone had already ripped her heart out and trampled all over it.

Don't get carried away, she thought to herself, anything could happen once Sage shows up.

Her mind just couldn't take all the new information the longer the time slipped by. She just wanted Sage to show up and reassure her that everything would be okay and explain what was going on. She wasn't sure exactly what he could say that could make the situation any better. He could say that the woman was lying and he didn't know her at all but why would she lie about it in the first place, what was there for her to gain? Did she really believe that Sage would drop everything he had to be with her? Mia wasn't sure. She hoped that after everything, their relationship truly was stronger than it had ever been.

After waiting for just over 20 minutes, the doors to the club opened and Sage walked in. It took all of Mia's strength not to walk over to him and kiss him, just to show Laura that he was hers now, but she didn't. Instead, she stood still by the bar and waited for Sage to make his way over to them. He looked from Mia to Laura with a confused look on his face. There was no recognition on his face whatsoever. Could it be possible that Laura was lying? Could her name not even be Laura or Lorraine?

"Mia, I thought you said Laura was here," Sage said as he stopped to stand next to her. He continued to look from Mia to Laura, not making the connection between what Mia had said on the phone. It just confused Mia even more. She turned to look at Laura who had lifted her head slightly, her body still hunched over the bar and her cheeks still damp from her tears. She didn't say anything nor did she make any move to go to Sage and tell him who she was. Why was she all of a sudden acting like a coward?

"This is Laura. She says her name isn't actually Lorraine like she told us the first time," Mia replied. She didn't know how she should act. She wanted to run out of the room and not have to deal with the situation at all but it was far too late for that. Sage turned his attention completely to Laura. Her head turned to face him, showing him her full face instead of hiding behind her hands.

Sage didn't react, he just continued to stare at her, his eyes never lifting from her face. Mia could see him look across her face, taking it all in, still not giving anything away as to what he thought. He didn't look at her the way he looked at Mia. He didn't look at Laura like he loved her. Mia had seen that he had been looking at her with love in his eyes recently and the look he had on his face did not look anything like that. Laura stood up from the barstool she sat on and walked slowly to Sage, closing the small distance between them. She leaned into him and brought her lips to his ear, whispering something to him, and it was only then that he reacted. His face lost all its color as his eyes widened. He was in complete shock and Mia was dying to know what Laura had said.

"We'll be back," he said. He wrapped a hand around Laura's arm, his knuckles white as his grip was tight, his fingers digging into her skin. She whimpered under his touch as he dragged her outside. She didn't look happy with the turn of events. She had clearly expected a different reaction from Sage and even Mia was a bit concerned by the look on his face. Mia wanted to protest, she wanted to shout and scream that he should not go outside with her, she wanted to scream 'No!' at the top of her lungs as she watched them leave.

The doors opened and closed as they walked out, leaving her there in a state of confusion and shock. What could be going on? She had no clue how she should feel. What did Laura say to Sage to get such a reaction from him, she wondered. Mia couldn't help but notice that Laura was a beautiful woman. She would be lying if she said otherwise. She had piercing blue eyes with dark chestnut hair, it almost looked black in certain lighting. She was the same build as Mia, maybe a little shorter but not by much. It didn't surprise Mia that Sage would be interested in someone like her. She was however completely different from Mia which she found to be a relief. At least he hadn't tried to find his ex in her.

She didn't bother going after them. She felt as if it wasn't her place to constantly stand watch over them as they talked. It really wasn't her place to get involved in the situation any more than she already had. If it was really Laura, a woman from his past, they would obviously have a lot of catching up to do. Mia took a seat at the bar, burying her head in her hands as she rubbed her temples with her index fingers. Her head had started pounding due to the situation and the fact that she was completely out of the loop. She didn't know what it could all mean. All she knew was that Laura still loved Sage and thought that he was rightfully hers. Mia could throw up at the thought of Sage and Laura hugging and talking outside, possibly gushing over memories from their past. She knew she had chosen a difficult man to love right at the beginning but she hadn't thought it would be this difficult. Surely when you meet the person you're supposed to be with, it shouldn't be so hard to be with them, because to Mia it felt like obstacles got constantly thrown in their direction every time things started to go right for them. Was it possible that they weren't actually meant to be together after all?

Her head continued to pound as her thoughts darkened while she waited for them to come back. Would they walk back into the club holding hands? Would Sage just turn around and leave her? She wanted to cry when she thought about it but she had to stay strong. Nothing had happened yet and her mind was just going into overdrive. There could be nothing to worry about, she thought.

"Mike?" she called. She slightly lifted her head so Mike could see her face. "Please can I get a vodka with cranberry juice," she asked.

Mike looked at her face, obviously noticing how fragile she looked.

"Of course, Mia. It's on the house too," he said before he turned away to make her drink. She knew everyone had seen the interaction between the three of them and everyone had seen Sage walk with the woman outside. The club was quiet. Everyone continued to talk in hushed tones. Mia could only imagine what they were thinking. She probably looked so weak to them and she was supposed to be their leader.

Pull yourself together, Mia, she thought to herself. Her drink was placed before her and she took a large sip just to calm herself down a bit. She needed to settle her nerves a little while she waited before she started pulling her hair out which she was very close to doing. She wondered if she should leave, if she should just meet Sage back at the house but she realized she couldn't do that without having to walk past them if they were still outside. It felt like she had already been waiting forever when in actual fact it had only been a few minutes.

She watched the clock tick by while she waited, counting the seconds, the minutes as they passed. How long would they talk for? She didn't know, but it felt like a century. She wondered what they could be talking about, what could Laura be telling him to make him see that it really was her. Mia had no picture of the Laura Sage had known so she couldn't know what exactly about her had changed and she wondered if Sage would be able to make out the person he once loved from the new version of her. Could their love be that strong that he could love her no matter what she looked like? From Sage's reaction, it didn't seem that way but maybe he had been convinced now that they were talking.

Mia hated how pathetic she was sounding to herself, how could she have become a woman who would go absolutely insane at the thought of losing a man. She knew she was stronger than that, but the love she had for Sage was almost so powerful it took over her rational thinking. She had to remind herself that it could be unhealthy for her to be so unable to see things logically. As much as she loved Sage she had to remember who she was. She would survive no matter what happened, even if that included a broken heart.

2

O nce Sage and Laura were outside, Sage could
finally do something. He didn't want to give
much away in front of Mia because he didn't want her to
worry about anything, and he knew she had nothing to
worry about. It didn't matter to him that the woman was
claiming to be Laura, he couldn't care less, but he didn't
want Mia to think that something was wrong. He
wanted to protect her from everything that had
happened, his past held nothing for him. He had let it all
go years ago and with the help of Mia, he had let Laura
go once and for all, which was why he was sure no
matter what happened, he would go back into the bar
and be with Mia.

He knew that Laura had died and there could be no
way that the woman standing in front of him could be
her. And even if it were, why would she have a

completely different face? He had been there when the bomb had gone off and he would always remember seeing it rip through his team before he blacked out. It was the hardest memory for him because for a long time, whenever he closed his eyes, all he could picture were the bodies of his team falling before him while blood gushed out of them. He could remember it clearly and before he had woken up in the hospital he thought it had happened to him. It had been the hardest thing to live through, having to remember the moment his entire team died, but he remembered it vividly and he knew Laura had been one of the bodies he had seen.

He knew it had taken him so long to move on from it all because of that, because he was just a few steps away from death, a few steps away from his team which meant he lived and they didn't. He knew that if they were closer to him it was unlikely that he would be the only one alive but that wasn't how things worked out and he had to accept that. This woman showing up and digging up his past just didn't feel good to him.

He didn't understand why she would change who she was and then expect people to just believe that she was who she claimed to be. It was obvious to Sage that Mia didn't have much to go on. He had never shared his past relationships or even any sort of photos of his past with her. Technically speaking he had burned most of his photos, especially the ones with Laura and his ex-military team. He didn't want to have any pictures around that reminded him of them any more than his memories did. The dreams he had been having for years were enough for him. He didn't need more photos to look at. The dreams he had been having had finally started to go away and he couldn't deny that he was worried that they'd come back now that his past was trying to ruin his present again.

He couldn't help but stare at her face, noticing that there were no marks, no scars and no clear sign that anything had happened to her face. There was nothing that indicated that any surgery had been done which just added more mystery to the situation. He looked into her eyes, which looked like Laura's. They were almost the same blue, the same piercing blue that always seemed to pierce into his soul whenever she had looked at him but although they looked almost the same, her hair was not the same color he had remembered. Her hair used to be black, the hair he saw in front of him was browner but could her eyes be the one thing that could tell him what she said was true?

He wasn't sure; he needed her to give him more information.

"Okay, you've got me here and you've got my attention. Tell me what the hell is going on and why you are claiming to be someone you're not," he demanded. He didn't want to believe that the person before him could be Laura, not after the time that had gone by and not after all the hurt he had had to live with.

"But I am Laura," she replied. Her face completely dry and her voice filled with emotion. Her eyes were wide as she stared at Sage, clearly wanting him to see her for who she said she was.

"No, you're not. Laura died. How could you be so cruel and pretend to be someone who died?" he asked. His voice shook with emotion. There was nothing in his body that told him she was telling the truth and it bothered him that she could do this so carelessly. It was disgusting how she could try to convince him that she was the person he once loved. It was horrible to think that someone could take her identity and use it in a sick game like she was.

"I am alive and I'm standing right here. I was taken in by a family after the bombing. They cared for me and kept me in Afghanistan until I was better. They became important to me, Sage, and they were all I had for a while," she replied. Sage could see tears started to well up in her eyes. The memory was clearly upsetting her, but he didn't buy it. To him, it just didn't make sense. Why had they even kept her?

"Why didn't they turn you over to the medics when they came for us?" he asked. He needed to know everything before he could even consider believing her. The story still didn't feel right to him.

"They were afraid to talk to the soldiers and honestly you can understand why. They weren't a threat and you know that if they had come out with a soldier, it could look bad," she stated.

He could understand that it could've looked bad for them. It could've looked like a hostage situation and that could've ended badly for everyone involved.

"But you were a soldier. Why weren't they afraid of you?" he replied. Laura did not answer right away. Instead, the tears in her eyes slipped down her cheeks.

"I was injured. There was no way I could've been a threat to them. Why can't you just be happy that I'm here, Sage?" she sobbed, her voice catching as the tears continued to run down her cheeks.

"Because I don't believe you," he replied and he really couldn't seem to think of any real reason why he should believe her. Her story had holes, big holes, and he didn't like the way she tried to brush over details.

None of it made any sense to him the longer he thought about it. There had been no news of anyone surviving the bombing and it didn't make sense that she would wait so long to come back into his life. He had grieved for Laura, he had beaten himself up every day for years because he hadn't been able to save her. He looked at her face again, still not seeing any sign that her face had been surgically changed in any way. He looked around her face, around her ears, forehead and chin, there were no scars to prove that something had been done to her face which just made the feeling in his gut grow more suspicious. Something wasn't adding up and he knew it.

If she had been alive all this time, why had she let her parents believe she was dead? How could she do that to her family? They had held a funeral for her. They had cried and cried as her coffin had been lowered into the ground. Who in their right mind would let their parents go through so much pain and then years later come back and claim that she, in fact, did not die after all? It seemed cruel and malicious to Sage and that wasn't the Laura he had known. She loved her parents and being apart from them had been the hardest part of being in the military for her. She had cried so much when she received things from them.

There had been so much time where she could've made herself known. She could have shown up on his doorstep right after she had been able to get back home and if she loved him like she had said she did before the bombing happened, he knew she wouldn't have wasted so much time to come back to him. He also knew he would've heard something, surely he would have, especially if she had been found alive instead of dead. Someone would have said that her body wasn't part of the remains that had been found and that was the biggest thing playing in his mind. Her body had been confirmed with dental records. How could they have gotten that wrong? Why hadn't she shown up at the military base with her new face and told everyone that she was alive? It wasn't as if everyone just left immediately after the bombing. She had time to come forward.

The more Sage thought about it, the more his head started to hurt. There were too many questions and warning bells going off in his head. He didn't want to deal with the situation anymore. He couldn't be around this woman. She reeked of alcohol and her crying was starting to annoy him. He wasn't sure why she was crying. If it was to seek sympathy from him it wasn't working. He couldn't just believe her so easily; he had to keep his guard up.

Laura or Lorraine, he wasn't sure if he would call her Laura if he wasn't sure if she was telling the truth, stood still in front of him. She didn't beg him to believe her, she didn't make any move toward him at all and all he could think about was the fact that Mia was waiting for him in the bar and he would prefer to be with her than with the woman who stood before him. He didn't want her to think he would leave her. He would never leave her but the situation did need to be dealt with and dealt with as soon as possible.

"I think you should go home. Get some rest and sober up. We can chat more about this tomorrow when no one is intoxicated," he said. He didn't want to be outside with her anymore, the smell of stale alcohol was too much for him.

"Okay, we can talk more tomorrow. I just want you to believe me. I'm telling the truth," she replied. Her tears had stopped and her eyes were red. He watched as she walked to her car, climbed in and drove away, looking sadly back at Sage before going completely out of view.

It felt like someone was playing a cruel joke on him and he couldn't stand it. He needed to ground himself before he even thought about going back in, back to Mia. He knew she would want answers and she most likely had a lot of questions but he just needed a moment to himself to breathe before he could face her. He stood outside the bar a little longer, thinking about all the things Laura had said. He tried to work out in his head if any of it could be true. He felt like that was highly unlikely but he also knew that it wasn't over just yet. He couldn't just let the situation go. He needed to find out what the hell was going on. He wanted to scream at the sky the more he thought. It was just all too confusing and frustrating for him. His past was supposed to stay where it belonged, not come back and try to claim him.

He wasn't an object nor would he happily leave Mia. If anything she had claimed him unknowingly. His heart belonged to her and he was happy about that. He had finally found someone who wouldn't give up on him even when he had been the worst version of himself. He took a few more minutes to himself, collecting himself before he turned and walked back into the bar. He knew he would tell Mia everything. There was nothing for him to hide and there was nothing inside of him that wanted to keep anything a secret from her. He decided that it would be the right time to finally confide in her, she had been patient with him all this time and she deserved to know everything she had been longing to know.

Sage wanted her to feel like there was nothing in his life he wouldn't share with her going forward. He was a completely new man because of her and he wanted her to know that his future would be with her. There was no doubt in his mind that no matter what happened he would stick by Mia and he just hoped she still felt the same. He could only imagine what she was going through as she waited inside for him.

He saw instantly when the doors closed behind him, her head lifted and turned when she heard the doors open, and the same happened with everyone else in the bar. It seemed that they had all been waiting for him to come back. Obviously, the drama hadn't gone unnoticed as he had hoped. Most of the guys nodded in his direction as he walked toward Mia. He wasn't sure if they were nodding with approval or just acknowledging him in general. The whole scene felt weird to him. He wondered what they all knew, he wondered if the woman had been saying all kinds of nonsense whenever she had been at the bar by herself. She could've been telling everyone her plan to take back Sage, but he hoped no one had believed her.

Sage noticed the worried look on Mia's face when she had turned to look at him, and all he wanted to do was make sure she was alright. He didn't want to be a part of her pain or worry. He only wanted to be part of her happiness because that was what she was to him. The role she had played in his life so far had been so much more than he had ever expected from his life. She had literally been a form of light and love when she had shown up in his life and that wasn't going to change on his account. Unless she one day turned and left him, he would constantly show her what she meant to him.

3

Mia stayed at the bar while Sage had been talking to Laura outside. She had started to worry that he had left her there. She really wasn't sure what was going on and she didn't know what he would do now that his ex had shown up out of the blue. Relief washed over Mia as she saw Sage walk back into the bar. She had turned around almost every time she had heard the doors open, wishing it would be him and finally it was. She had her second drink in front of her. She had to have something to calm her nerves before she lost her mind while waiting. She had started to drive herself crazy as the minutes had ticked by.

Once she saw Sage walking over to her, she turned her face back to face the bar, staring vacantly at the bottles that were displayed before her. She didn't want to say anything until Sage did. She didn't want to make matters worse because she had no idea how he was feeling. She could only guess what was going on in his mind and even then she could be terribly wrong. She could hear his footsteps on the ground. The sound got louder as he got closer and her heart went crazy in her chest. She took a sip of her drink to distract herself. She had to remain calm.

Sage sat down next to her. He didn't say anything at first. Instead, he called over the bartender so he could order a drink for himself. Mia could tell that he looked worn out. His eyes looked drained and confused as he stared off into nothingness. She didn't want to be the first one to break the silence so she continued to sit next to him quietly. Both were lost in thought as they sipped their drinks. She wanted to ask him so many questions. They were all on the tip of her tongue but she held them back. He would talk to her when he was ready.

"Let's go home," he said. They had both finished their drinks. Mia felt better that he was going home with her; she wouldn't have to be alone. He reached out and took her hand as they stood up and made their way to the door. She didn't pull it away but she didn't hold his hand tightly either. She didn't know how to feel or act until they had talked about everything.

Sage called them a taxi and they both sat silently in the back. As much as Mia wanted to break her silence, she didn't want to start the conversation in the back of a taxi. The silence was almost deafening during the ride home. Once they arrived home and were a bit more comfortable, Mia asked the first question on her lips.

"Who is she?" she asked. She didn't want to wait any longer and waiting wasn't helping the situation either. She had held her tongue for as long as she could. Sage looked at her, taking one of her hands in his, he led her to the couch.

"Let's have a seat. It's going to take a while to explain everything," he replied and for the first time in his life, he wanted to tell someone everything. He had never wanted to share his past with anyone but because he loved Mia, he wanted her to know everything.

"There's a lot about my past that I haven't told anyone and that's just because I've always believed that it's something that not everyone needs to know and then I met you and for the first time I want to share my past so I'm going to start from the beginning," he said. Mia didn't say anything in return. Instead, she just nodded her head, confirming that she'd listen to his story. She was happy to hear that he would tell her everything. She had been waiting for the day when Sage would open up to her and although she wished it hadn't been because of the current situation she was happy nonetheless.

It wasn't just that he was sharing his past, it was bigger than that for Mia. It was him showing her that he trusted her enough to tell her everything. She felt as if she had finally proved to him that there was nothing that would keep her away from him. As long as he stuck by her side, they could face anything together. The love she felt for Sage grew stronger in her chest. The man of her dreams was opening up to her and it meant more than words could ever say.

"Obviously, you know I was in the military, and during that time I met Laura. It was something I had never planned for but she was such an amazing person and because we shared so much time together, it was hard to stop myself from falling for her. Laura and I started to get to know each other and we fell in love. We had a whole life planned for when we would get back from the military. That had been the first time in my life that I had thought about a future. I had never met anyone before her that made me believe I could settle down and have a family, but that changed when we went out on a mission one day," he said. Mia watched him as he spoke. She could see the emotion on his face and she could hear it in his voice. It was clear he had loved her. She could never take that away from him nor would she want to. A person's first love would stick with them forever and she could see that Laura had been important to him.

"The mission was supposed to be quick, an in-and-out kind of job but nothing really works out that way." A sad and cruel laugh escaped his lips. "On that day, the worst possible thing happened. We had been trapped. We were ambushed by men with guns who started firing at us with no avail. It escalated so quickly after that." His voice choked up as if the air from his lungs had disappeared and Mia noticed tears building in his eyes. She knew it was hard for him to talk about his past. He had tried for so long to avoid it and seeing him so cut up pulled on her heartstrings. She could understand why he had tried to keep it to himself. Having to relive something so traumatic couldn't be easy for anyone, even an ex-military man.

Mia wanted to reach out and wrap him up in her arms but she stopped herself so he could finish his story. It was also important for him to talk about it. She could only guess what kind of pain he had been through while he had kept his past buried deep inside of himself. It must've eaten away at him for years and only now he was able to talk about it. Going to the military on its own would be huge for anyone to deal with but being ambushed and almost killed would make it so much worse for anyone involved.

"There was a bomb that went off. It came out of nowhere and left only shattered lives in its wake, my life and the lives of the families left behind. You see, I was the only survivor," he said. Mia didn't know what to say. She hadn't expected anything like that. It was bigger than she had thought had happened. She tried to picture herself in his shoes and her heart just broke even further.

"I was then airlifted out of the area and had to face the fact that my team didn't make it. None of them would go home, not alive anyway, and that was the hardest thing for me to accept. I suffered a wound to my head, I'm sure you've noticed the scar," he said as he looked at her, a slight smile on his mouth. There wasn't much about Sage's body Mia hadn't noticed. She had spent hours staring at him, she had traced her fingers over his skin over and over again. She knew his body just as well as she knew her own. She smiled tenderly at him, nodding her head slightly so he knew she had noticed his scar before.

"I was lucky. I couldn't believe everyone was gone. I couldn't believe that all I had to show from the bombing was a scar on my head and the rest of them… The rest of them were taken. It was so hard trying to look at it as a blessing because it didn't seem that way to me. I've never felt grateful for it, especially considering Laura had been on my team and was taken too," he said sadly. Mia realized that Laura had been very important to him. She could hear it in his voice and see it in his eyes.

"The woman at the bar is claiming to be someone who should be dead and I honestly believe she is lying. I couldn't see any signs that there had been any surgery done to her face, there were no scars which would obviously be visible if she had done something to change her face," Sage said.

Mia thought back to the woman's face and also remembered not seeing any scars or marks on her face which wouldn't make sense, just as Sage suggested. The situation just became a lot more confusing for Mia. She didn't know what to make of it all because if the woman was lying, she must not have a kind bone in her body. No one in their right mind would just go around and lie about something so personal. And if she was lying, what else could she be capable of doing? All kinds of questions filled Mia's mind.

"I want you to understand that no matter what this woman says, there is no way I'm leaving you. This right here," he gestured to her and then back at himself, "is what I want. There is no one else I want to be with other than you." Mia felt relieved to hear Sage say what she had been hoping he would say. She didn't want to be the type of person who would demand him to reassure her but she was glad Sage had felt the need to tell her anyway.

There was nothing more he wanted to say. He had told the story of his past and he just wanted to be close to Mia. He pulled her into him so he could hold her in his arms. He wanted to feel the warmth of her body against his. It brought comfort to him through all the mess that surrounded them. Mia was a little stiff at first, not completely giving herself to him, but soon she gave in. He had told her everything and she believed he had been honest about it all. Of course, it still played on her mind and she wasn't sure what would happen going forward, and even though he had been very stern with how he felt, if the woman ended up convincing him that she was Laura, it could change everything. He didn't believe it was her which was why it was so easy for him to say what he did but if she was Laura, what would happen then?

"Laura is in the past, and yes, I did love her. I loved her very much but I've let her go," he said against her hair as if reading her mind. He was really trying to tell her that she didn't have to worry and it helped ease her mind a little.

"Are you hungry?" he asked. Mia pulled away from him so she could look at him. He looked calm and relaxed, as if nothing could phase him. It made her feel better instantly. She realized that she hadn't eaten much but she wasn't hungry either. The emotions in her body had kept her distracted from any form of hunger.

"Surprisingly no, I'm not hungry at all," she replied.

"Neither am I. It is a little late though so why don't we head off to bed?" he asked. Mia hadn't noticed the time. Although she had been watching it at the bar she hadn't actually been paying attention to the actual time. It was already after 10 pm.

"That sounds like a good idea," she replied. They got up off the couch and Sage led Mia to his room.

"Will you spend the night with me?" he asked. His voice was soft and gentle as he looked at her. It was hard for Mia to say no so she agreed to spend the night with him and followed him into his room.

He curled his body against hers as he fell asleep, wrapping her up in his arms for comfort. It didn't take long for him to fall asleep while Mia stayed awake against him. His breathing came and went softly as he dreamt and Mia thought that he must be emotionally exhausted from the day they had had. She knew it must've been extremely taxing for him, as it was his life that had been ambushed more than Mia's. Although she was involved with Sage, it wasn't her past that had come back with a vengeance. She was certain that Laura would not go quietly. She had already made her presence known and the likelihood of her just giving up and walking away seemed slim.

Sage already knew that he would make sure Laura knew that there was no chance of him leaving Mia for her. He didn't even love her the way he had. That part of him was gone, he had set it free when he had let Mia in. No part of him belonged to Laura anymore, he was completely void of all feelings for her and he felt like there was nothing wrong with that. If they had broken up properly, he would still have the same feelings as he did. He knew he would have to make sure Laura understood that they couldn't and wouldn't be together. He had gotten a tattoo of a lioness for Mia and would prove that he was not up for grabs.

He slept surprisingly well that night. He didn't feel as if there should be something to be concerned about. Everything would be sorted out and back to normal in no time. He dreamt of Mia, breathing her in as he slept. The smell of her skin was reassuring, knowing that she was there just made him sleep that much better. He had no fears of the future. He was sure that the person who claimed to be Laura had been paid a huge amount of money and that was the only sickening part of it all.

4

The look of pain and loss on Sage's face stuck in Mia's mind as she felt him breathing against her skin, sleeping peacefully at her side. She would never forget how his voice had sounded so pained as he told her his story. She knew already that he was strong but his true strength showed as he opened up to her, trusting her with something that had hurt him for so long. It meant a lot to Mia that he had opened up to her but she wished it had been under different circumstances.

She wished she could take away his pain and she wished she could erase his past from his memory just to spare him of the loss he had suffered. Losing a loved one of any kind would be hard but losing them on the battlefield must've been harder because that would be a memory that would never leave a person's mind. Mia hadn't lost anyone to death before. She had walked away from her family so many years ago, she didn't even know if her mother and father were even still alive. Her mind went back to the few days she had thought Sage had died and that brought so much pain to her but she knew it couldn't compare to the pain Sage had lived with.

He hadn't just lost one person that day, he had lost his entire team and Mia knew that in the military your team becomes your family too. It couldn't have been easy for him to wake up and realize that they hadn't made it. Her heart really did break for Sage. She wouldn't wish that kind of pain on her worst enemy. She knew she wouldn't have been strong enough to live after something like that. She could remember the number of times she had questioned her own life and her pain couldn't even be compared to that of Sage. She had willingly walked away and left her loved ones behind whereas Sage didn't even have the choice.

The story of Sage's military experience played over in Mia's head long after he was sleeping. Her heart ached for him and the pain he had gone through. She couldn't believe he had suffered something like that all on his own. He had suffered in silence for so long and he had pushed it so deep within himself that he had made himself believe that he was fine. Mia knew he wasn't fine, she had known all along and a part of her was relieved that he had shared his past with her. He had been so vulnerable in front of her, she had wanted to protect him so much. She wanted to protect him going forward but she was unsure about what would happen with Laura being back. How would it change the future she had pictured for herself and Sage?

She laid next to Sage as he snored gently beside her. She knew she wouldn't sleep any time soon so she decided to go to her paint room. Although she wanted to be next to Sage because there was nothing better than having him next to her, she didn't know if she could just stay next to him until tiredness took her.

Her mind was filled with too much, all the information she had learned about Sage just played over in her head. She couldn't deny that there was still some sort of worry in her chest when it came to Laura. Although Sage had reassured her that there was nothing to worry about, she still couldn't think about possibly losing him.

She got up quietly and made her way to her favorite place in the house, the one place she could go to and not feel too much. She could just let everything go. She looked at all the pictures of Sage she had painted over the past few weeks and it made her heart ache even more. What if everything changes from here, she thought. She didn't want to think about it and she didn't want to touch the paintings of Sage. Instead, she took them one by one and moved them, placing them in one corner of the room. She didn't want to look at them either. It was just too hard and too painful for her to look at the gentle face she had painted. To her, his face was almost that of an angel's and with their lives hanging in the balance, she didn't want to look at them.

Instead, she reached for a blank canvas, one she could pour her emotions on. She needed to start fresh, from scratch, so there was nothing that could take away from all the feelings she had. She needed to release them the only way she knew how. She realized that Sage wasn't the only one who found it hard to talk about feelings because Mia struggled with it too. Although she had tried to show him how she felt there was still a lot that she hadn't said out loud. She knew she would have to tell him eventually, so he would know exactly how she felt.

She doesn't reach for any brushes either as she felt like she needed to touch the paint and connect with the canvas so instead, she dipped her fingers into her paint pots, letting her fingers paint her feelings. Soon her fingers just started to create their own pattern as she painted, letting herself completely go.

She was overwhelmed by her emotions as she started to paint. Her heart ached not only for Sage but for herself. She had been in love with him for so long and now it could all be ruined. She had no idea what her future looked like and for once it looked so out of reach that she wasn't sure if there was anything she could do to get it back onto the right track. It wasn't up to her, nothing was her decision. She couldn't control Sage and what he did, all she could control was how she handled herself. She wanted to break down but she knew that wouldn't help. There was no point in crying, she knew that, but she also knew that it could help her get the knot out of her chest that had started to get bigger the minute she had learned who Laura was to Sage.

She didn't want to let herself go back down a path of sadness with the thought of Sage and Laura being together. It had to be enough that he had told her he wasn't going to leave her.

She still wanted to cry though and she could feel the tears build in her eyes. The hurt and pain were almost too much for her so she continued to paint. Her fingers drew lines and soon mountains and valleys came to life. Greens, browns, and blues all started to mix together, it was completely messy while sharp ridges started coming through as well as smooth planes. She didn't care that it was a mess though, she didn't care that it hardly made any sense and there was no pattern behind it all. All she cared about was getting her feelings out and for a moment it made her feel slightly better.

The painting wasn't something she would paint freely. It wasn't her style because it was completely abstract but she liked it. She had never been someone who conformed to the way society saw things, she didn't want to live her life in a box that someone had set for her which was why she broke almost every rule placed before her and the thought of her life broke her heart. She tried not to think about it, she tried not to let her mind wander back to Laura, the first love of Sage's life because even though she had been his first love, Mia wanted to be his last. She wanted to be with him no matter what but she couldn't help wondering if they would make it through what had happened now.

What if this woman really is Laura, she thought, would that mean Sage would go back to her? She didn't really believe that but a part of her wasn't sure either. She didn't want to believe that Sage would leave her so easily, not after everything they had been through. Of course, it hadn't been as big as the military and surviving that but they had gone through their own ordeals that had made them stronger and closer than ever. Could that be enough for them to work past it all? Mia was sure it meant something, it had too. She was overcome by emotions as she stopped painting and stood still in front of her work. Tears began to run down her cheeks as the sinking feeling of losing Sage became stronger.

She didn't want to move, she didn't want to go back to bed with Sage and she didn't have the energy to go back to her bed either so she fell to the floor. She grabbed the sheets that she had laid out on the floor and wrapped them around herself before bringing her knees to her chest. She wrapped her arms around herself, making herself as small as possible as the tears became thin and heavy, weighing her down even further. She didn't want to break and she didn't like the fact that she was crying over a man but she had let herself lose herself completely to Sage and the thought of losing him was too much for her to handle. She wasn't sure what she would do if she had to say goodbye to him, if he decided to leave. She didn't want to picture her life without him and that made it even worse for her as she fell asleep to the thoughts of losing Sage to a woman who had been the first person he had loved.

"You know you're stronger than this, right?" a voice said to Mia. She turned and came face to face with her mother. It was clear that Mia had called upon her while she slept.

"Mommy," she breathed. The child in her felt love and joy as she looked at her mother for the first time in years.

"Come here, my darling, everything is going to be okay," her mother said as she stretched out her arms and beckoned Mia to her. She stumbled as she reached for her mother, resting her face in her chest as she wrapped her arms around her. Her mother closed her arms around her and held her close to her, stroking her head with her one hand.

It was such a comfort to Mia. She had missed her mother for the longest time.

"Do you really think I'll be okay?" she asked, her face still buried in her mother's chest.

"Yes, my dear, you are so much stronger than you think and I wish you would realize that for yourself," she replied. Mia didn't move as she savored her mother's touch. She felt like a child again and her mother was there to protect her.

"But I don't feel strong. I feel so weak and useless," she said, a sob escaping her lips as she cried as she had never done before.

"Oh, my dear child, you are not weak and I wish you would stop telling yourself that you are. You have gone through so much and look at you still standing through it all," her mother insisted. Mia thought about what her mother was saying and she knew deep down she was right. She had been through so much in just over 10 years and she had constantly put herself down. She knew she could be stronger and that she should be stronger but she felt incredibly tired.

"I'm just so tired of it all, there always seems to be one thing after the other and I can never catch a break," she huffed. Her mother let her go and placed her hands on the sides of her face, cupping her face like she would've when she was a child.

"That's just how life works. Nothing is ever perfect and you should never expect it to be either. Life is crazy and beautiful. Yes, it is also hard and sometimes miserable but when you look at all the good things you have and focus on that, nothing else *really matters. You need to focus on the good in your life, my dear child, only then will things seem better," her mother said. She knew her mother had a point. It all made sense the longer she thought about it. Yes, there were a lot of things in her life that seemed to be uneasy and completely out of her control but there was still so much she could be grateful for. She looked at her life, and she noticed that she still had so much going for her. She had the Hell Kats and the Screaming Demons, she still had Fiona and Grier on her side and even with the uncertainty of it all she still had Sage. Her life wasn't as bad as she had made it out to be. She had a lot to be grateful for.*

"Thank you for making me see things in a clearer light," she said with a smile. She felt like she could face anything and even though it wasn't real, she was grateful that her mother had come to her and made her feel better.

"I'm always here for you. I just wish things could be different," her mother said.

A part of Mia knew what she was referring to and she knew she would've wanted things to be different too but it was too late now.

"Me too, Mom, me too. It hasn't been easy for either of us," she replied. As a teenager, she had always wished her mother had been more accepting of her but the version of her mother she had created in her dream was not the true version of her mother.

There was no way they could ever rebuild their relation-

ship and there was no hope for them to ever really be a normal family after all. Mia had always known that.

She sat with her mother a bit longer. They both sat in silence as they enjoyed the moment they shared. It would end soon for Mia and the child in her that had never grown up with her mother would have to let go of the hope that things could ever work out for them.

They sat on a bench, facing a sunset that had appeared before them. Mia rested her head on her mother's shoulder and closed her eyes.

"I'll miss you," she said. Sadness filled her heart as the sun set completely before them and it was goodbye.

5

*S*age looked over at Laura who stood before him. She had rosy cheeks with a huge grin on her face. She was dressed in a white dress that made her skin glow as well as her hair.

"How are you doing, Sage?" she asked as she looked at him. Her face soon looked confused as she took in the look across his face.

"I'm just really confused. I felt like we had let each other go but you seem to always come back," he said, frustration filling his voice. He already knew he was dreaming. The Laura in front of him looked nothing like the Laura he had seen a few hours ago when he had been awake.

The person before him was the Laura he remembered. Her face was framed by her black hair and her blue eyes sparkled in the light.

"What do you mean I keep coming back? I mean I don't

ask to be in your dreams, Sage," she replied defensively. They had both gotten used to the fact that they would meet in his dreams and they had both been completely aware that it was just a dream.

"I know that, Laura, and that's not what I'm talking about. There is a woman that has shown up and is claiming to be you," he said. He shook his head as he finished his sentence. He was still in shock about what had happened.

"Well, that's impossible. We both know I'm dead, Sage. I didn't make it. You don't believe her, do you?" she asked.

Sage knew he would be stupid to believe the woman who was claiming to be Laura.

"No, I don't believe her. I remember what happened and from my memory, there is no way she could be telling the truth," he replied. It was hard for him to speak like that to the person he had always hoped had made it out despite all odds but he knew and so did she that it wasn't possible.

"I'm truly sorry this is happening to you, Sage, it can't be easy for you and I wish there was something I could do. The only thing I can say is that whatever that woman says to you is a lie and you should not believe her for a second," she said. Her voice grew sterner as she finished her sentence, making sure he understood how serious she was about it all.

"I can promise you now that I won't believe her. There are just too many flaws in her story." Sage went on to explain the story she had told him while Laura sat wide-eyed in front of him. Once he was done, a laugh escaped her lips.

"That story sounds so ridiculous," she said as she tried to keep more laughter from coming out of her mouth. Sage smiled at her, also becoming aware of just how ludicrous the story sounded now that he had said it all out loud.

"It does sound extremely crazy, doesn't it?" he said. And the more he thought about it the bigger the joke became. It was a cruel joke but one he could in no way take seriously. He knew that when he woke up he would have to set the record straight. But while he was with Laura in his dream they continued to chat and joke around. Carefree and happy.

He woke up more sure of himself than he had when he had gone to bed. He knew in his heart that Laura had died and no matter what anyone said, there was no way she would've shown up now with a completely new face.

Sage woke up to an empty bed. He could understand that everything that had happened could be too much for Mia. He just hoped that she wouldn't think too much of it. There would be no reason for her to worry, he would never leave her, especially for someone who claimed to be someone she most definitely was not. Sage still couldn't believe that the woman who claimed to be Laura could actually be Laura and he would prove it, not only to himself but to Mia too because he knew it would ease her mind.

He decided to leave her. He didn't want to disturb her because he knew she would need her time and space but being apart from her really didn't feel good to him and he wanted to be with her. He realized more than ever that he wanted to be with Mia and even if the woman really was Laura, he wouldn't leave. He had loved her in the past, he couldn't deny that, but he had moved on and he had earned the right to be happy with someone after all the time he had spent grieving which was a lot longer than he had thought it would take. He had cut himself off from feeling anything for anyone for so long after the bombing, he had held onto the guilt and pain of it all but he had finally found someone he could picture a future with. A new future, a future that he could have more control over and one that wouldn't just disappear in front of him. He knew he wasn't ready to think about marriage and kids but it could be something he'd be willing to talk about later on. He could picture himself having kids with Mia, he knew he loved her that much.

He sat in the kitchen thinking while he drank his morning cup of coffee. He had denied himself of true happiness for so long that denying himself any longer just seemed too stupid. He didn't want anything to keep him from living his life the way he wanted to. He didn't deserve to have all of his hopes and dreams snatched away from him just as he had accepted everything.

The thought of being with Mia brought a smile to his face and he knew he would have to sort out the Laura mess as soon as possible so it wouldn't become a problem for them. He didn't like the fact that Mia had been so distant and withdrawn the night before. He knew she appreciated him being honest and open with her, he could see it on her face before they went to bed, but also knew that she was threatened. He had seen it in her eyes when he had explained he had loved Laura and he had felt it when he tried to hold her. Even after she had sunk into his hug she had been reserved, stiff and almost cold. He could understand why but he didn't want them to backtrack. After all, it had taken a lot for them to get to where they were and he would hate for that to be ruined.

He started his shower, allowing the hot water to steam up the room before he got in. He savored his shower as he allowed his muscles to relax beneath the hot water. The tension had already started to build in his back and shoulders and he wanted it to be gone. He tried not to let himself get worked up all over again. It wouldn't do anyone any good, especially him when he had a mystery to solve. He knew he had to play his cards right. There would be questions he could ask that could give him the answers he needed and if Lorraine messed up at any point he would know for a fact that she wasn't Laura. He knew he didn't need to know if she was being truthful or not, a part of him didn't care. He had moved on from his past and had let it go but he wanted to make sure that once he closed the door on his past, there were no stones that were left unturned.

He stepped out of the shower, toweled himself dry and got dressed in a white shirt and black jeans. He wanted to look like he was ready for business. He would not take the situation lightly at all and he wanted Lorraine to see that. He walked out of the house, locking up behind him so he could make sure Mia was safe in his absence. She was still nowhere to be seen when he left. He got onto his bike, needing the opportunity to feel free as he rode his way to the bar. Unlike Mia, he had no idea where Lorraine lived so he would have to get her address from someone at the bar. Someone should know considering she had been there a few times. Maybe Mia hadn't been the first one to take her home after one of her drinking benders. The thought of Lorraine drinking also didn't sit well with Sage. Laura had never been a big drinker when he had known her so it didn't make sense that she would now spend most of her time getting drunk at a bar all by herself. He allowed himself to remember some of his past, just enough so he could use it to help solve who the woman was and why she had shown up.

He didn't want to think too much about his past, it had been too much for him to work through and he didn't want to have to deal with it all again. The thought of remembering small and intimate details about Laura was already changing his mood. He needed answers and he needed them quickly. His life had turned around for the better and the thought of Mia ignoring him broke his heart. There was no way he could go around the situation other than talking to Lorraine. She was the only person who held all the answers and as he entered the bar to ask Mike if he had her address, a sense of dread came over him.

He had a quick conversation with Mike before he thanked him for Laura's address and then made his way to her house. He needed to find out more information from her before he accepted anything she said.

He knocked on her door and was greeted by a much more sober-looking woman. She didn't smell of alcohol and she didn't look like she was a crazy drunk. She was an attractive woman so it confused Sage that she would try to pretend to be someone else other than her true self.

"Sage, I'm so glad you showed. I was getting worried you wouldn't come," she gushed as she let him in.

"I'm not here because I believe you so don't get your hopes up. I'm only here for more answers," he said. His voice was stern and strong; he didn't want to play any games.

"Of course, I understand," she replied, "you can ask me whatever you want."

She gestured for him to take a seat on her couch

while she sat down on the couch opposite. He thought it wise that she was keeping a certain distance between them.

He had a few basic questions in mind that he wanted to ask her.

"What's your favorite color?" he asked.

"Blue, the color of your eyes, of course," she replied. He remembered how much Laura used to say she loved blue, the blue of his eyes and the blue of the sky.

"How old are you now?" he asked.

"Thirty. We just celebrated my 25th birthday before we were deployed," she said. A smile lit up across her face. Again, she was right. He had tried to make it the best birthday party he could've. It was hard being away from family during that time and he wanted her to still be happy even if it was away from everyone she loved.

"What was the name of your first dog?" he asked. Sage knew it was a trick question; he needed to see if she slipped up with her story.

"I've never had a dog. I've never been a fan of them. I've always wanted a cat," she replied.

However she had gotten her information, she had made sure to learn everything she could. It was almost scary when Sage thought about it.

She had a look of triumph on her face as she saw the look on Sage's face. She could tell she was getting all the questions right and the chance of her lying seemed to be fading before them. Sage didn't want to believe it and there was one last thing he could bring up that could make or break everything. There had been a mark on Laura's stomach, a brown blob that was about an inch wide. It was a birthmark and although she had always hated it, Sage had found it different.

"Can you show me your birthmark?" he asked. He didn't say where because she should know but at the mention of it all the blood in her cheeks disappeared.

"Haven't I done enough, Sage?" she asked angrily.

"Just show me your birthmark and then it's all over," he demanded.

"No, I won't show it to you. You loved me so much once, you don't love me now? Why can't you accept that it's me? I love you, Sage, you're what brought me back. Please, don't do this," she begged. The warning bells in his head went off. He couldn't let it go.

"Show it to me," he demanded again. She puffed air angrily out of her mouth before lifting up her top. Her stomach was clean, with no birthmark in sight. Something like that couldn't be removed so easily though, again there would be some sort of visible scar to show it had been removed.

"I hated it so much, I got it removed," she admitted. He didn't believe her. All of her lies had finally caught up with her and there was no way she could get out of them.

"I don't believe any of your lies. The only way I would believe you is if you give me your fingerprints so I can test them, then you'd have nothing to hide," he said. He could see tears forming in her eyes as she realized she hadn't won him over yet.

"Sage, please," she whispered. He wasn't having any of it. He wanted her fingerprints so he could only then know for sure if she was truly Laura.

"If you want me to believe you, you have to give me more proof," he replied. Begrudgingly she stretched out her hands so Sage could take her fingerprints. He had thought about it beforehand and had brought a small stamp and a blank sheet of paper so he could make sure he got a good print. He placed three of her fingers in the ink and blotted them on the paper. He took three samples just to make sure that if one didn't work properly he would have more to work with.

6

Mia knew she was being really dramatic over the whole thing. It wasn't Sage's fault but a part of her blamed him for making her feel the way she did. She knew it was completely irrational and there was no room to blame anyone but the woman, whoever she was. Mia knew in her heart that Sage was over his past. He had told her that and she could tell he meant it but the irrational side of her just kept telling her that she had every right to worry.

The room was cold and all the curtains were drawn. Mia looked around her and noticed a room void of all its furnishings, holding only a few paintings on the walls.

Her surroundings didn't make any sense to her. The room wasn't a room she knew and the paintings seemed to be hers. She could make out her name scribbled in their corners, but none of them seemed to be anything she remembered painting.

There was no pattern to the paintings and there didn't seem to be any deeper meaning to them either. One painting was just different colored circles overlapping each other, creating a never-ending cycle. Mia stood before her paintings, trying to see what the deeper meaning could be, but none of them pulled any emotion from her. They didn't feel like her normal paintings. She usually always felt a connection to them but for some reason, there was nothing that connected her to the paintings in front of her.

These can't be mine, she thought, and why is the room empty? It was all confusing to her. She soon realized what it all meant. It was her life without Sage.

He wasn't in any of the paintings and there were no paintings that symbolized their relationship either. She had painted meaningless and emotionless paintings because she had no meaning in her life. She turned around the room and found herself alone. There was no one and nothing that indicated that she had a family of any kind. Her heart ached at the thought. She tried to make herself wake up, you're only dreaming she thought but as hard as she tried, she continued to dream. It was scary for her to think that her life held no meaning without Sage in it, and it wasn't just because she loved it but it was also because she believed that if he left, Fiona and Grier would rather keep him around than her which also didn't help the ache in her chest.

This isn't real, she said to herself, Sage is still with you and you need to stop thinking like this.

While she slept she tossed and turned on the floor of her painting room, moaning in her sleep as her body started to get covered in a thin film of sweat.

There was one painting that caught her eye in the far corner of the room. It was the painting she had just painted while she was awake. She could see the mountains and valleys she had just drawn. She knew then that she was right about what the dream meant. The shock of it all brought her back to a conscious state as she screamed for Sage.

"Sage!" her body rocketed awake as her eyes shot open. She was panting and sweating as if she had just run a marathon. Her emotions were running wild while she remembered her dream. It was all too much for her as tears started to build up in her eyes once more. Her eyes already felt raw and tender from all the crying she had done the night before, she didn't want to start all over. She already knew her face would be puffy and there would be no hiding the emotions she had, especially if she saw Sage. She would break down all over again and yet she ached to be with him. She didn't like that she had slept without him. Even though there was so much going on and she needed her space, she had gotten used to sharing a bed with him.

She felt pathetic for getting so overwhelmed over something that hadn't happened yet and something that may not even happen. Sage had shown no indication of leaving her for Laura, he hadn't shown any emotion to her whatsoever besides reliving his past which after all was just the past. She tried to remind herself of that as she laid on the floor. She wasn't ready to move and she continued to stay on the floor for a little while longer until she couldn't take the hardness of it against her skin any longer. She wanted her bed and she wanted Sage.

Mia got up off of the floor, stretching her body as it screamed at her. It wasn't a wise decision to sleep on such a hard surface. Her body wasn't prepared for it as it hurt almost at every joint. She would have to soak in a hot bath to hopefully help ease the pain. She searched for Sage, going to his room to see if he was still sleeping only to find the bed empty. She did a quick scan of the house, but he was nowhere to be seen. Had he left to go to Laura? Mia wasn't sure but part of her guessed he would have done. He also had a lot of questions and he wanted answers. He wasn't going to get the answers from anyone but Laura or whatever her name was. Mia still wasn't convinced it really was Laura but it wasn't something she could prove.

She wanted to phone Sage to find out where he was but she didn't want to seem needy or clingy. She had never been the type of person who would act like one of those girlfriends who didn't trust their boyfriends. She had seen how those types of relationships crashed and burned faster than lighting a match. There was no way she would become that person, especially when it could drive Sage away in the long run. She couldn't risk it but she remembered how he looked when he spoke about Laura and it was clear that he had loved her. Mia didn't want to compare her relationship to his past relationship but she couldn't help but wonder if he loved her the same or even more. What she would do to have him love her that much.

Mia's body ached as she walked through the house and so she decided that she would have a bath after all. She wanted to relax her body and hopefully relax her mind. With Sage out of the house, leaving nothing for her to work with, she wasn't completely at ease. She just wanted to get out of the house but decided not to move in case Sage came back. She wanted to know exactly what he had been up to. She felt like she sounded a bit crazy, she sounded like one of those girlfriends who stalked their boyfriends and wanted to know their whereabouts all the time. She couldn't become that person, she was better than that.

She spent some time in the bath with her eyes closed, trying to make her mind relax. It didn't work and soon she hopped out of the bath so she could make herself breakfast.

After cooking and eating her breakfast, her mind wandered back to Sage. Thinking about him and his past relationship wasn't doing any good for her; she needed to do something to distract herself. There had to be a way to find out more information about Laura. She still had a strong suspicion that the woman was not who she said she was. None of it made sense to Mia and she also didn't want Sage to get his hopes up. Being tricked into believing someone from your past is still alive when in actual fact they aren't could be the hardest thing to deal with, Mia thought. She made her way to her laptop. There was only one way she could help and that was by doing her own research. She typed in the name that Sage had given her. It was the only lead she had and it would have to be the one thing she worked with. An obituary popped up on her screen.

She read through it and her heart saddened at the thought of a young woman's life being taken from her so young. She had been Mia's age when she had died. It was an awful thought. Thinking of death so young scared Mia because for once she was happy. Mia went back to the main search, reading all the sites and links that had popped up during her search. There were a lot of sites that wanted people to pay a certain amount of money before they could view or access any more information that had been posted. Mia didn't want to pry too much so she decided to stick to the sites that were free and tried to gather as much information as she could. The one thing she had noticed was that there hadn't been any reports of a soldier who had been declared dead who was actually still alive. It was reassuring to her that the story the woman had told Sage didn't have any traction.

There was nothing at all that led her to believe that the story was true. There was nothing mentioned that she had come back and declared herself alive. Mia found the original report of Sage's incident while she did her research. Her heart broke as she read through it. She even saw a few photos that had been taken of him while he laid in the hospital. A huge bandage had been wrapped around most of his head. He looked so small and fragile in the photos, Mia's heart ached for him. At the thought of Sage, she wondered when he would be back. She really wanted to share her information with him.

She continued to glance through the reports that came on her screen. She also glanced at the sites that asked for money. She tried to see if there was anything she could take away from the site without having to pay. She then noticed a list of relatives, a sister was listed and that was it. Either her parents didn't want to be involved or they weren't alive either. Could it be her sister that had come back claiming to be her? Why would she do that, why would she claim to be her dead sister? It was a sickening thought and Mia wanted to throw up the more she thought about it. It seemed like a sick game that just didn't make any sense.

She just wanted Sage to come home the longer she

stayed at the house by herself. She took to watching the time tick by once again, just like she had at the bar and waited for Sage to come home. She wanted to share her information but she was also worried that something had happened to him. The last time he had vanished he had ended up being stuck in a well for three days and close to dying. Mia freaked that something like that had happened again. She tried to keep herself calm. It was highly unlikely that something like that would happen again. She just had to wait patiently for him to come home.

It was driving her crazy, she was driving herself crazy. She tried to go back to her painting room so she could paint as it wasn't often that she would have the house to herself. She turned on some music and tried to distract herself with her art. But it all fell flat as she stood in front of her canvas, unable to paint anything. It had never happened to her before but she knew why it was happening. Although she was emotional she had gotten most of her feelings out already, there wasn't anything left for her at that moment. She just wanted everything to go back to how it was when everything had been simpler and happier. She felt as if she had a dark cloud hanging over her head as she walked throughout the house, finding anything she could that would distract her from her thoughts and loneliness.

She tried to clean for a while. It usually calmed her

when she had been stressed in the past but the more she cleaned the more frustrated she got. Nothing was helping her and nothing was easing her mind. She was irritable and angry the more the day passed by. Whenever she had gotten into a mood like that she knew it was all in her head, even as she looked at the time she noticed that it was still early and Sage couldn't have been gone that long at all. She irritated herself more than anything because she wanted to be herself again, she didn't want to be so frantic and wound up but she also couldn't help it. There was no way she could ignore what was happening. It was not only affecting Sage's life but her life too. She had fallen in love with a man who had a horrible past and it seemed that together they just had horrible luck. It didn't stop her from loving him and wanting to be with him, of course, it just made their lives a lot more complicated than they really needed to be. Mia supposed that was the biggest problem. Nothing had run smoothly since they had met and all she longed for was some sort of normality. But she thought that to be almost impossible the more time passed. Their lives didn't seem to have anything normal about them.

She then decided to work out a bit while she waited. She thought that exercising would help relieve her of some of the tension in her body and it would also be a good way for her to release her pent up energy. She hadn't worked out in days and it showed as she tried to do her normal routine and slowly started to lose incentive throughout the workout. Once she was done with the workout, she hopped into a quick shower and went back to her computer, hoping that she could spot something else that would help the situation. She scrolled through the websites again, taking her time to make sure that she didn't miss anything. She bookmarked any of the sites that she felt held something they could work with. Any details that could point them in the right direction would be a start. She was so zoned in on her computer that she didn't notice that Sage had arrived back home. She stayed glued to the screen.

7

The woman had been a little reluctant about giving Sage her fingerprints but in the end, she did what he asked. It was the only way he could be sure of the truth. He didn't have much to go on. Although she had known intimate details, she still didn't have the right face nor anything else that proved she was Laura. Once he got her fingerprints, he made his way home to Mia. He wanted to make sure that she was alright and didn't feel too worried about the new arrival in their lives.

Back at the house, he found Mia hunched over her computer, her face buried behind the screen as she read whatever was on it. Sage stood quietly for a while. She hadn't noticed him yet so he took the opportunity to watch her for a bit, taking her all in and memorizing her face. He could stare at her all day if he was given the chance. After a few moments, Mia shifted in her chair, and lifted her face, noticing him for the first time.

"Have you been staring at me for a while?" she asked, her eyebrows raised with suspicion.

"Just a little while," Sage replied with a small chuckle. Mia didn't say anything in return. Instead, she remained still, staring at Sage with a questioning look. He knew it wasn't about him staring at her. She wanted answers as to where he was and what was going on. He knew she trusted him but he also understood that if roles were reversed he would also be worried and concerned. He knew that if he were in Mia's shoes, he would be freaking out. There was no way he was ready to lose her.

He closed the distance between them and pulled her into his arms. He wrapped his arms around her, holding her tight against his body.

"Everything is going to be okay, I hope you know that. I'm doing everything I can to sort out this mess. We'll have the answers we both need soon enough," he said while resting the side of his face on top of her head.

"I know, Sage, I trust you," she replied. Hearing Mia confirm that she trusted him made him feel so much better about the situation. With her by his side, he knew they could work through anything that got thrown their way.

"I'm so glad to hear that. I managed to see her this morning. I was going to come and find you before I left but I thought you might want your space. There are a few things that aren't adding up for me so I got her fingerprints which I'd like to send to Fiona. She could probably get them tested and identified for us," he said. He didn't really want to bring Fiona into the situation but he had no other choice. She knew people he didn't and that could help them get the answers they needed.

"That sounds like a good idea. Hopefully, she can give us more answers. I've also found a few things but I'll wait for you to finish talking to Fiona before I tell you what I found," she replied.

With a nod of his head, Sage let go of Mia and reached for his phone in his back pocket.

He dialed Fiona's number and after a few rings she picked up.

"Sage, I feel like there's something you need," she said, skipping the pleasantries. Sage knew she must have been getting used to being called when there were emergencies. Luckily he had managed to sort out a lot of things without her but this time he would need her help.

"Hi, Fiona. I wish I was calling under better circumstances but you are right, I need your help," he replied. He quickly explained the situation to her, explaining that it didn't make any sense and he had a fingerprint he needed to be tested.

"Well, I know a few people who could run it through a database. You're right though, it doesn't sound right so with that said I want you and Mia to be on full alert. We can't let anything slip by us," she said and Sage completely agreed. They didn't need any more nonsense and bad shit happening around them, although it seemed to always happen that way.

"Completely agree, we'll be careful. In the meantime, I'll scan and capture the fingerprints and get them sent to you immediately. Thank you for your help, Fiona," he said.

He didn't know where he'd be if it weren't for her. He'd most likely be lonely, wasting his life away. He shuddered at the thought.

"We're a team. I'm also going to get hold of the number for her parents. It might be a good idea for you to speak to them directly. They might have answers too," she replied. Sage had already thought about talking to her parents but also knew that it would be a hard topic and a hard conversation that he would much rather avoid. He hadn't spoken to them since the funeral that was held for Laura. They probably didn't think very highly of him.

"Yes, I was thinking about that too. Thanks, Fiona. I'll keep an eye out for your message," he said. The line went dead after that. Fiona had never been the type to say goodbye when a conversation was done.

Sage thought about what he could say to Laura's parents. He would have to be very careful with how he phrased his sentences. Until they knew exactly who the woman was, he couldn't mention it to Laura's parents. He couldn't risk getting their hopes up that there had been some sort of mistake only to crush them in the end. He wouldn't be able to live with himself if he did that, even if it was unintentional. They had been very good to him when he had met them, they were kind people who deserved more than a dead daughter. He sometimes thought that they hated him for what had happened. He knew there wasn't much he could've done to change the way things went but maybe they blamed him for not helping her, for not moving her out of harm's way. He wished he could've. It was one of the things that ate away at him.

He made his way back to Mia who had stayed in her office while he had been on the phone. The look on her face was very aloof, as if she was trying not to act very interested. It was obvious that she was interested though. He could tell she wanted him to tell her everything.

"How did things go today?" she asked. Sage could tell that she didn't want to pry but it was only fair that she knew what he had found out. He explained the news to her, telling her that he had gotten fingerprints because he still didn't believe her story.

From the very beginning, he hadn't believed her. Outside of the bar, her story had seemed to be fake and made up with so many holes in it. And then the story about her birthmark just made everything seem even more far fetched. He remembered that Laura had hated the birthmark. She had always complained about it whenever he had seen her shirtless but she had never expressed the need to have it removed. He could tell that when he had asked to see it the cracks in her story started to show. It clearly wasn't a question she thought he would ask. It was a very personal thing but he had known about it and it was the one other thing that really reflected who the woman was, and she most certainly was not Laura.

"There's something that just doesn't sit well with me. I know she's lying but I just don't understand why. Like what does she have to gain from it all? That's the part that confuses me the most, none of it makes any sense to me," he replied.

"I'm glad you said that. I managed to do a little bit of research while I was here and I found a few sites that say she had a sister. It got me thinking that it could be her?" Mia said.

Sage thought about it for a while. He played back in his mind some of the family discussions he had had with Laura and he couldn't remember her at any point mentioning a sister.

"I honestly don't remember her ever saying she had a sister. I was thinking it could be another family member, a cousin maybe," he suggested. He still couldn't be sure what the game was, what the aim of it all could be. He had never gotten the chance to meet Laura's family besides her parents but it also didn't make sense that her cousin would do something so cruel to him. He had done nothing to the family. The more he thought about it the more he realized that could've been the problem.

Maybe someone was doing this to him to make him pay emotionally for the hurt he had caused, maybe someone blamed him for the death of Laura and hurting him was the only way they thought revenge could be had. Maybe they wanted to plant her in his life just to remove her again but even that sounded too far-fetched because the woman still looked nothing like Laura. He couldn't wrap his head around it and the possibility of it being a relative made the situation much worse.

It didn't make sense that a family member would pretend to be a dead person. That just didn't seem alright with him and he didn't want to believe that someone in her family could steal her identity like that. How could her own family be so heartless? As far as Sage could remember, Laura had never said anything bad about her family. She loved them and she had always seemed like one of the favorite members in the family from all sides. Sage remembered the letters she used to get from her family, they had always seemed so full of love and concern for her well-being.

"Why would someone in her family try to pretend to be her though?" Mia asked. Sage smiled slightly at her question. The one thing he loved about her was how quick and smart she was. There were hardly any details that got past her. It was as if she took note of everything that surrounded her, and he found it fascinating and absolutely amazing. He also knew that was one of the reasons why she was so sure he was telling her the truth. She would pick up immediately if he were lying and she would call him out on it. It was one of her best characteristics.

"I was just asking myself the same question. It just doesn't seem like a very family thing to do. Someone would have to super fucked up and cruel to steal someone else's identity," he said shaking his head while the gravity of the situation sat on his shoulders.

Mia nodded in agreement. Both of them were left speechless as all the possible reasons and ideas went through their minds.

On some level, Sage believed that they were missing the bigger picture. There was just something so fishy about the situation that it almost seemed to be more than they could possibly imagine. He couldn't believe that a family member would do something like that and it didn't seem like Laura was actually alive. There had to be some bigger reason that neither of them was seeing. Sage could almost sense that they were just scraping the surface with the questions and ideas they were bouncing around. He didn't want to see the woman anytime soon, he didn't want to be anywhere near her. It felt like a pending doom had been placed on his head. Something big is coming, he thought to himself.

"The whole situation just confuses me, there is nothing that makes sense. Nothing that she says or does reminds me of Laura," he said. He watched as Mia's eyes flickered from his face to the ground. He could tell that the conversation was too much for her. It hurt her still and he couldn't stop it and he couldn't take it away until he knew what was going on. He would have to wait patiently for Fiona to get back to him with more information from the fingerprints which he hoped would come back with more answers.

He tried to push all of his thoughts out of his head. They had begun to go round and round, making him even more confused. He didn't want to think about it and he also knew that Mia surely didn't want to talk about it anymore either. Of course, it was a problem that they needed to solve but until they could find out more, they were stuck with the information they had.

Sage stood behind Mia at her computer. He stared at the screen with the story of Laura written all over it. It could be easy for anyone to read the story and cause drama with the people left behind such as himself. Reading the story of the bombing made it all too real for Sage, it cut at him. He couldn't stand that someone had taken the life of an innocent soldier who had lost her life trying to save the country so they could use it to play some cruel game with him. It was disrespectful and honestly disgusting. No one deserved that, especially Laura after everything she had done. She was a truly amazing person who had been taken too soon. She still had so much life in her and so many dreams she still wanted to achieve. It was hard for Sage as he saw a picture of her face on the site. She had a huge grin on her face while she wore her uniform. She looked happy and excited about life. It brought tears to Sage's eyes the more he looked at the article. He had to turn away before Mia saw how emotional he was getting. He knew that if she saw him cry it would not ease her mind.

He wasn't crying for Laura just because he had loved her but because her life had ended so abruptly. There was no chance for her, there was no future for her and whether her life included Sage or not, no one would ever know. He had grieved for her, and he had grieved for his team and he hated that it was all coming back to him. Whoever was behind all of it would pay and Sage would make sure of that. No one should play with someone's life just because they are not around to say anything about it. Sage, however, was around and he would definitely do something about it.

8

———

After discussing the situation with the woman a bit more, Sage and Mia decided that for the remainder of the day they would just try to have a good time with each other. It seemed a bit unrealistic but they had to try. Their lives had been filled with so much drama that they just wanted to forget it all for a while so they could just enjoy each other's company.

The time they had spent together recently had been very awkward and tense and until more information was brought to their attention they wanted to push it from their minds. Until everything made sense they didn't want it to bother them too much. It had already started to form a wedge between them and they were both unhappy about that. After all, they had both just gotten tattoos to signify how strong their bond was.

They both knew that it would only be a momentary

space for them to have some time to themselves. Soon they would have to face the music and sort out the situation at hand. It didn't seem as though the situation was going to go away anytime soon though so it wouldn't do them any harm to just put it on hold for a while.

"I think we've had enough Laura talk for the day. Let's do something fun and relaxing," Sage said. He could do absolutely anything with Mia and enjoy their time together, it was one of the effects she had on him. It had been a while since they had spoken about anything but Laura and neither of them wanted their lives to revolve around her. They both deserved to be happy and because they made each other happy they could afford to ignore the world for a while.

"I completely agree, what would you like to do?" she asked.

"Well, I'm slightly hungry so why don't we make something to eat and then we can see what's on TV? I don't feel like going out right now," he replied. He much preferred to be wrapped up in a little bubble with just Mia. Just the smell of her perfume drove him crazy.

With a smile, Mia led the way to the kitchen and Sage followed close behind. The kitchen was spotless and Sage remembered how neither of them had really eaten much for the past couple of days. There had been so much going on and so many feelings involved that neither of them felt hungry enough to cook. Sage looked down at his body and he could tell he had lost a bit of weight over the last couple of days. He knew he needed to eat so he could keep his strength up, especially if he wanted to protect Mia.

"Is there anything you feel like having?" Mia asked. Sage watched as she looked in the fridge and all the cupboards noting what they had available.

"I'll eat anything that's placed before me," he replied, which for Sage was true. He had never been a fussy eater. Sage also knew that whatever Mia cooked would be amazing. He had tasted her cooking so many times that he knew she had a way with cooking. No matter what she cooked it always came out tasting almost restaurant quality. Mia pulled out a packet of pasta, a jar of pasta sauce, some cheese and then all the pots she needed. Sage stayed still by the doorframe, watching Mia as she moved through the kitchen. He could watch her for hours, she moved so gracefully and effortlessly that it was almost captivating to watch. She moved as if she floated, it hardly looked like she touched the ground as she moved from this side of the kitchen to that side.

"Are you going to watch me all day?" she asked, catching him staring at her. She smiled at him, letting him know she was just teasing.

"I could honestly watch you all day, to be fair," he replied. He moved toward her to help, filling the biggest pot with hot water so it could be placed on the stove for the pasta.

"You're incredibly weird," she said with a small laugh.

Her laugh sent off all of his emotions, as if he was falling in love with her all over again. It was crazy for him to think that through all the drama she had stuck by his side. He truly loved her for all that she had already done for him and he knew he would spend the rest of his life making sure she knew just how much she meant to him.

It was easy for them to fall back into how they normally acted around each other, especially after the recent growth of their relationship. They were both pleased that the day had taken such a good turn. Neither of them wanted anything to do with Laura at that moment and that wasn't because neither of them cared about the situation but it was because there was nothing they could do about it.

Once Sage placed the pot on the stove, he reached for two wine glasses, pouring them a small glass of wine each.

"I know it's still early but I think we both deserve it and considering we're not going anywhere, there isn't any harm in a small glass while we have lunch is there?" he asked with a wink. They weren't going to get drunk so early in the day but having a drink could definitely help lighten the mood.

"I think we both do need it. It's been a crazy few days," she replied, taking a sip of her wine.

"I think that when this is all over, we should go away for a while, get a break from all the drama. What do you think?" he asked. He wasn't sure if she would agree but the thought of them going away sounded good to him. They had both been through so much in such a short period of time that getting away from it all sounded like something they both needed. Mia stood quickly, not taking her eyes off of the pot which had started to boil. She carefully placed the pasta in the water, sprinkling salt and a bit of oil with it so it wouldn't stick together.

"Hmm, that does sound like a good idea. Hopefully, this mess can be sorted out soon. I can't imagine how hard it is on you," she replied. Turning to face him, her eyes filled with concern. Sage's heart grew as he saw how much she cared for him. If it were a better moment, he would have told her right then that he loved her but he wanted that to be special, not in the midst of some crazy woman showing up and trying to ruin everything they had built.

All of a sudden, Sage heard yelling coming from outside their gate. It sounded like a woman and he had a feeling he knew who it was before having to even look. He peeked through the kitchen window and saw the woman. He hadn't decided which name he would call her considering he didn't know who she really was yet.

He couldn't make out what she was yelling but she was definitely asking for attention. He didn't want to give it to her but there was no way around it. Mia stopped what she was doing, taking note of the noise coming from outside too.

"I guess our wishes for a quiet day together are ruined," she said. Sadness washed over Sage as he watched the light in her eyes slowly disappear. He hated what the woman had done and he couldn't stand to think that Laura could be doing it. It didn't seem like the kind of thing she would ever do to him. If she were alive, he thought, after all this time, she would've let him live in peace.

They made their way outside and watched in horror as the woman started yelling at them through the gate. Neither of them could believe she had shown up at their front door, and not just that but had shown up completely drunk again. It seemed to be a regular thing for her.

"I think we need to go out there and try to settle her before the neighbors complain," Mia whispered to Sage.

"Are you sure?" he asked.

"We don't really have a choice, do we? We'll go out together. That way neither of us is alone," she replied as she placed her hand in his. Sage smiled at her and pressed the button to open the gate. Laura stopped shouting almost immediately and didn't try to move toward them as they made their way to her.

"Sage, why are you still with her when I've come back for you?" she asked, her voice filled with sadness. Sage couldn't take it. He couldn't understand why she would act like that.

"You need to leave, you're not wanted here," Mia said, stepping forward so Laura could see that they were a unit.

"No! You should leave! You're not the one he wants, he wants me!" she yelled back, throwing herself at Sage. Mia couldn't believe what she was seeing. She watched as Laura leaned into Sage and tried to kiss him. Sage moved his head and quickly pushed her away.

"No, you can't do that," Sage said. His voice was strong and authoritative.

He could call the cops on her and get her removed but he didn't want to get them involved. They never got the cops involved in their business.

He pulled out his phone and called Adam while Laura sat slumped on the floor where she had landed after Sage had pushed her. He hadn't meant to push her that hard but he had acted fast and he couldn't control his strength.

"Hey, Adam, you busy, mate?" he asked down the phone. "Awesome, can you come and remove Laura from my property?" he said. "Thanks, mate, see you soon," he said before hanging up the phone.

"Adam is going to come and collect her. I can't handle this," he said to Mia.

He looked at her face and could tell she couldn't handle it either. She looked extremely angry and he hoped she wasn't angry with him since he had pushed Laura away before she could actually kiss him.

Within minutes, Adam pulled up in front of their house. He walked Laura to his car and gently placed her in the back seat. He didn't say much before he climbed back into his car and drove away.

Sage couldn't stand that Mia was so angry, he took her hand and led her back inside.

"Shall we try to carry on with our lunch?" he asked. His voice was gentle and soft. He didn't want to irritate Mia.

"Ahh, yeah, I think we should try. The pasta should be done as well," she replied. Her voice came out in a daze and she didn't look at Sage as she made her way to the kitchen. She finished cooking the meal and dished up a plate for each of them. Sage could see her eyebrows were knotted together through most of the meal, which they ate in silence. He didn't know what to do. Their day had just started to get better and it seemed that it had done a complete 180. Once they were both done, he quickly cleared away the plates. He didn't want her to worry about a thing. She stayed seated at the dining table and he couldn't take the silence anymore. He moved toward her, gently placing a finger between her eyebrows to soften her face.

"I'm sorry," he said as he kissed her forehead, and then kissed her cheek. "I'm so sorry," he said again, desperate for her to loosen up. She turned her face and looked at him. It was an impulse move as he reached forward and kissed her lips, gently and softly. It took a moment for her to respond and soon her lips were kissing him back. A sense of joy went through his body as he pulled her up off of the chair so he could pick her up in his arms, lifting her feet off of the ground as he cradled her, still keeping his lips locked on hers. He carried her back to his room. All the tension from earlier was completely gone and only the raw sexual passion was left hanging in the air.

Once they made it to his room, Sage planted Mia back onto the ground, pushing her against one of his walls so he could be as close to her as humanly possible. Their tongues entered each other's mouths as the kiss grew deeper, the sexual frustration they had both been feeling had reached a boiling point. Mia reached for his shirt, lifting it up and over his head and Sage followed her lead. Within moments they both stood naked in front of each other. Sage took the opportunity to kiss her. He kissed every inch of her body, remembering the freckles that he had missed so much. He gently picked her up and placed her on the bed. He didn't want to tease her because he wanted her so badly and he didn't want to be too rough either. He wanted to savor the moment, he wanted to make love to her.

Their mouths connected once more before Sage reached for his bedside table. He pulled the drawer open and retrieved a condom. He moved his hips so they were between her legs and she looked at him with lust and love. The look on her face was almost his undoing. He moved slowly, edging his hips closer to her and as he finally met her, it was almost too much for them both as he moved deeper inside of her. She moaned with pleasure as he moved until he was all the way inside of her. He groaned in response, completely focused on her body and the way she felt. He was on cloud nine as he wrapped himself around her, her legs wrapped around his waist in return, keeping him close to her as his hips dipped. They moved together, both almost close to unraveling at the same time. Mia moaned his name and it was all he could take before he moved faster and harder, needed to release. Her moaning grew higher as the pressure built deep within and in a moment of unison they fell apart, both completely taken by ecstasy. Both of them were a mess, breathing heavily and uneven as they collapsed into the bed, into each other.

9

They were a crumbled mess on Sage's bed. Neither had gotten their breathing back to normal as they came down from their high. The room smelled of sex and sweat as they laid crumbled on top of each other, as if they were a deck of cards someone had stacked and then proceeded to blow over. Mia laid her head on Sage's chest, feeling his heartbeat beneath her. They were happily wrapped up in each other and in their own little world again. It was magical and better than anything that had happened recently. Once their breathing went back to normal, they listened to the rain that had started beating against the window. It was calming and relaxing, especially as the cool air made its way through the windows and into the room, cooling them down.

They both stayed silent as they listened to the rain.

Mia closed her eyes as she lay peacefully on Sage's chest. It was all she had wanted and so much more. He had shown her just how much he cared for her. She had felt it in every kiss and every touch. It wasn't just about the sex, it had been so much more than that. It had been about them being close and connecting on an intimate level again. It had been a while since they had been so close to each other. They had shared a bed together but it was moments like that which made their bond that much stronger.

She wouldn't have minded staying there with him for the rest of the day. She could get up if she needed but the feeling of having him next to her was all she needed to calm the storm that had started to rage in her heart and mind. Nothing mattered to her anymore, nothing that had happened recently weighed down on her. As long as she had Sage and they were together, they could get through anything and even though she had known that at the beginning, she had been reassured by him when he had pushed Laura away from him. It was clear to Mia that he had no intention of being with the woman and it was a relief to her. She had tried not to think that he would leave her but she supposed that any woman in her position would've thought the same.

"This is good, you know, this is how I want it to be," Sage said while he traced his fingertips across Mia's skin, creating patterns and sneakily writing words of love and appreciation onto her skin. Mia sighed at his touch, melting into him.

"I want it to be this way too, just you and me," she replied and her voice was filled with love, Sage could hear it.

"I think we should get out of here and I know the perfect place to go. Clearly staying at home just brings people here," he said. Mia nodded her head in agreement and slowly lifted herself off of Sage so she could shower. Sage got up soon after she walked out of his room so he too could shower. The last thing they needed was to shower together. That would only go one way and just the thought of it turned Sage on once more. He was wildly attracted to Mia and he knew that the attraction he felt toward her would never go away. Just the way she moved turned him on.

After having a steamy shower and once changed into a fresh green polo shirt and a faded pair of blue jeans, Sage made his way to Mia, just wanting to be near her again. He was pleasantly surprised when he saw her. She had changed into a beautiful baby blue dress which only reached mid-thigh, making his mouth water at the sight of her.

"You are too beautiful for your own good," he teased as he glanced over her body, taking in all the curves that were emphasized by the dress. She blushed at the compliment, covering her face slightly with her hands so he couldn't see. It was a tight-fitting dress, hugging at her hips so perfectly. He almost wanted to take her back to his room but stopped himself. He wanted to take her out and away from everything if only for a few hours. As much as the situation was hard for him, he knew it was also hard for Mia and he wanted her to know that she still came first for him and no one could change that.

He had noticed over the last few days that the light in her eyes had started to fade, as if she had started to lose faith in her life and in him. It made him sad that she would feel that way and he wanted more than ever just to make her smile and feel better. It was important to him that she smiled, that her eyes sparkled because then he knew he was doing something right. He wanted to give Mia the life she had always wanted, the life she had always dreamed of. He didn't want to cause her sadness. He knew it wasn't exactly his fault but he had to change how the rest of the situation played out. He couldn't risk doing anything that could potentially make Mia leave him. He needed her just as much as she needed him. He had to be better for her, stronger and kinder. He wanted to treat her better going forward.

He took her hand and led her out to the car he had recently bought. He knew Mia had been looking into it too so he decided to surprise her. He wanted to do something for her that would make her happy and this had been the first step he took in that direction.

"What is this?" she asked as she saw the car. He could see the shock and surprise written all over her face. He was chuffed with himself that he had gotten away with it without her suspecting a thing. It made the surprise that much better.

"It's our car. It's been a while since either of us has driven anything besides a bike so I thought it would be as a good time as ever to finally get a car, with the help of Fiona, of course," he said. His face beamed with pride as he noticed the shocked look on her face grow even bigger. She had not suspected a thing with all the drama going on, especially since the car had arrived while she was still getting ready. He had picked up that she was tired of riding the bike and that getting a cab all the time was also starting to annoy her. It had also started to annoy him too which is why he decided to get the car. It was something they both needed but he also knew that getting something she had wanted just showed her how much attention he paid to her and her needs.

"That's so thoughtful of you, plus you beat me to it. I had also started planning on getting a car," she said with a small laugh. He had already guessed that when he noticed more car ads popping up on his computer, which meant they were being searched for regularly.

"I know you were so I thought I would beat you to it," he said with a wink. He opened the passenger door for her and gestured for her to climb in. "Your chariot awaits, m'lady," he joked. She laughed and climbed in. Sage was happy to see her smile and laugh again. It brought him joy to be the reason she laughed. It would always be music to his ears.

"Where are you taking me?" she asked once Sage closed the door after getting into the driver's seat.

"There is a diner I know of that could be the perfect place for us to be on a day with weather like this," he said with a grin. The rain had picked up slightly but it had stuck to a calm pace. There wasn't any wind but just a gentle breeze.

He pulled the car out of the driveway, making sure to watch the gate close completely before driving away from the house. He was excited to be with Mia, somewhere where no one could find them and they wouldn't be bothered by any drunks. He wanted her all to himself, he wanted to remind her that nothing had changed for him and no one could change how he felt for her. He wanted her to know by not only his actions but also by his words. Of course, he had gotten a tattoo for her but he also wanted to tell her that he was hers and that wouldn't change anytime soon, possibly for as long as they lived. He had always been scared of expressing himself but Mia had brought that out of him and he wanted her to know that his life had changed completely because of her. She was the best thing that had happened to him and he was ready to tell her that.

They drove in silence to the diner. Sage had one hand wrapped around Mia's hand on her lap as they drove. He felt at peace. He knew the diner would be perfect. There was a screened porch that had a porch swing that they could sit on and watch the rain. It would be exactly what they needed. They arrived at the diner moments later and Sage could see the smile on Mia's face as she looked at it. He could tell he had made the right choice.

"Don't move," he said as he parked the car and got out of the driver's seat. Mia hadn't as he walked around the car and proceeded to open her door. He was being a true gentleman. She smiled as he reached a hand toward her and helped her out of the car.

"Oh, you are so amazing," she said as she stood on the pavement outside the diner.

He took her hand and led the way, taking her straight to the porch so they could claim the swing. A waiter came over to them and handed them both a menu.

"We don't need these," he said and he handed them both back to the waiter. "Could we please have two of your homemade doughnuts and two cafes au laits," he said with a grin. The waiter nodded and walked away, leaving them alone.

"You're lucky I like you so much or else I would kill

you for ordering for me," Mia said jokingly with a wink. Sage laughed in return.

"You're not that tough when it comes to me, maybe with other people but not with me," he teased as he lifted her hand to his mouth and gently placed a kiss on her palm. She shoved him gently.

"Don't be so cocky," she said.

Sage laughed once more and pulled her into him. He wrapped his arm around her shoulders so she could rest her head on him. It was what they needed to relax. Neither of them had realized just how much tension had built up between them while they had been at the house together.

They had been walking on eggshells, neither of them knowing what to say or do around the other. They needed ever so badly to get out of there, they needed to break from it all, even if it was only for a moment. It was peaceful being there. They sat in each other's company blissfully content. They didn't need to talk the whole time. There was no reason for it as just being around each other was enough for them.

They gently pushed the swing, rocking it to and fro as they sat quietly and watched the rain pour down around them. Soon their waiter placed their order on a small table in front of them. They sipped on their drinks and slowly nibbled away at their doughnuts.

"These are so good," Mia said halfway through a

mouthful of her doughnut. Sage was glad she liked it. He knew she would but he was grateful she had assured him that he had made a good call.

"God, you're the only one for me, Mia," he said after watching her for a while. He felt overwhelmed by love and the word sat on the tip of his tongue. Mia looked at him, her eyes wide with shock. He knew she hadn't expected him to say that. "I just want you to know that there is no one else for me, only you," he said. He lifted up his hand that had the tattoo on it. He wanted to remind Mia that is wasn't just a tattoo, it was a symbol of just how much she meant to him.

"I don't regret getting this tattoo, not a single bit. It's not just for you but every time you look at it, I want you to remember that you are the one for me," he said.

Mia touched the tattoo and took in the details of it again. It was healing and it looked perfect. It still shocked her how genuine he was. He meant every word he said and she knew it. She leaned in and kissed him. It was a kiss that was filled with passion but nothing too much considering they were out in public. She looked into his eyes, letting him know that she loved him and he could see it.

"No matter what happens, no matter what gets thrown at us, I am here and I am here to stay. I'll always be here for you," she said. They both knew that she meant it because she had proven time and time again that she would not give up on him and she would not give up on their relationship.

Sage's heart grew bigger in his chest. He knew he could never be away from her and he would never allow anyone to take her from him. He would protect her and look after her for as long as he lived and that would be the greatest thing he could do with his life. She was another gift that had been given to him, a gift to help him see the true meaning behind his life and he could never take that for granted. After a few hours of sitting at the diner, they decided to head home. They couldn't avoid it forever but also because they had talked to each other and opened up a bit more, they both felt good about going home.

10

To Sage, one of the biggest things that had plagued him had been the thought that he would never have someone he could call family. He knew his real family was still alive but he wanted a family of his own. When he had tried to think of a family that didn't involve Laura, it had been hard. After all, she had been the first person to place those kinds of thoughts in his head but with Mia around, he could finally see the light at the end of the tunnel and it was her. He wasn't sure how the situation could get resolved any time soon but he knew that his life was better with Mia in it.

He hated to admit it but it was a much better life than he had had with Laura. He had always wondered what would happen once she got bored which she so often did in life. There were so many things she changed about her life almost all the time and the only constant had been the military. Once that was removed, she always wondered what she would do. If she would stick to her dream of studying again or if she would've gotten over that and found something else to do. He didn't want to think negatively about her and he hated himself for doing it but it had played on his mind since he had lost her.

Sage lay next to Mia that night and held her body close to his as she slept. He felt so content just being around her and the time they had spent together had been the perfect break for them. Just having her close to him made him happy and peaceful but he couldn't help but think about the woman. He couldn't fall asleep with the thought of her still being out there and causing trouble. The fact that she had shown up drunk at their house and tried to kiss him sent warning signs off in his head. He was still waiting for news from Fiona and the unknown of it all ate away at him. He kept thinking about her, more out of irritation than anything else. He wanted her out of Florida. There was already enough evidence for him to believe that she was lying about who she was. Although he was still waiting for confirmation, he was sure she was not Laura.

He was frustrated that the relationship he had with Mia had almost been on the edge of crumbling because of this woman, because of someone who claimed to be his ex-lover. It was frustrating that she had come out of nowhere with all her claims because even if it was Laura, which he didn't believe was true, he didn't want to be with her anymore. He belonged with Mia and that was what made him happy, she made him happy. He looked down at her sleeping body as he thought about how happy she made him. She looked so peaceful and comfortable, all he wanted was to make sure that she was always happy. He had pushed her away for far too long and now he would spend the rest of his life showing her what happiness could be like.

He had loved Laura once, he truly had. He could never deny that nor would he even try to deny it and he'd always remember their relationship but it was over and there was no going back, and he knew that even if he could go back, he wouldn't. When he had been with Laura it had been amazing, their relationship had been crazy, hot and passionate, filled with love and happiness but that changed when he got back from Afghanistan because he had come back alone. Laura had died and he believed now that she was in fact still dead. It hurt to think about it, especially since he had let her go, but she hadn't made it back and that was the fact of the matter. He had loved her when he had been a completely different person, but he was not that person anymore. The person or rather the man that had loved Laura had also died. He had died when he realized he had no one left.

He had to bury the young hopeful man he had once been when his life had crumbled in front of him. It had been one of the hardest things he had had to go through and that didn't change just because Laura might be back. It didn't change the way he felt and it didn't take anything away from Mia and the role she played in his life. He knew that when he had chosen his tattoo for her that that was his way of signing himself to her. He didn't belong to anyone but her. Obviously, he still belonged to himself since he still had to keep some kind of wits about him but he knew that Mia was it for him. There would be no changing that. Nothing could take him away from her.

It was hard for him to think about the person he had once been just two years ago. It seemed like almost a lifetime ago to him. He had been so different and yet so similar to who he was now. He had been so hopeful about life. Naive would be a better word, he thought. He used to believe that everything had a balance in life, as if saving one life could change the way everyone acted. That definitely wasn't true. No one cared so much about the art of living, no one cared about anything but them-selves. Sage had watched people kill each other over the smallest of things and to him, that wasn't a balance at all.

He had been so stupid to believe that being in the military would change the world because two years later the war was still going on. It seemed to never end. No one was satisfied with what they had and they always wanted more. They could kill for more, slaughter the innocent for more and the world continued to work based on greed. He had come out of the military knowing for sure that he would never be the same person he had been before and he was actually grateful for that.

It had taken all of who he was to rebuild himself, rebuild himself stronger than he was. He never realized how weak he was as a person before he had gone on his mission. He was just too young and even though he was 27 at the time, he still believed he didn't have enough experience at the time to really understand what it was all about. He had damaged himself in the process of trying to fix himself, making it harder for him to love anyone ever again but that was until he met Mia.

She had changed him, changed him into someone he could be happy with looking at in the mirror. He felt more emotions than before, he had more faith and he believed that he did, in fact, deserve to be alive. She had given him the reassurance that he had needed to believe that his life meant something and he didn't need to feel guilty for surviving. He didn't want to go back to his old life, thinking about a life without Mia just didn't feel right to him. He knew he would do anything for her, he would kill a dozen or more people just for her if he had to. He would protect her with his own body as a shield if he must, he would die for her.

He knew he would've died for Laura too, he really would've placed himself between her and the bomb if he could've but he couldn't change the past and the past all of a sudden coming back up didn't change the future either. He knew without a doubt that even if the real Laura had shown up, he would not go back to her. It wouldn't do him any good and he never wanted to be the cause of any pain when it came to Mia.

The feelings in his chest grew the more he thought about it and soon Mia was all he could think about. The words 'I love you' wanted to spill out of his mouth. He wanted her to know that he loved her because he already knew she loved him. He had seen it for so long and he was finally ready to admit to her that he felt the same. He hadn't said those words in years and the thought of saying them had been daunting to him but not anymore. He knew that the minute she was awake he would tell her. He felt that she deserved to know that he had something he loved for the first time in a long time and it was her. He leaned down and kissed the top of her head while she continued to sleep. She sighed at his touch and her eyes started to flutter open. He didn't mean to wake her up. She usually slept through almost anything. It was a complete surprise that she had stirred awake so easily. Sage thought that maybe on a subconscious level she had been worried that if he moved it would mean that he was leaving her and it had woken her up so she could react. He didn't want her to worry about him leaving her because he knew that was her biggest fear. He still had to prove to her that he would never leave her.

Shit, I've woken her up, he thought.

He wanted her to go back to sleep. She had been so peaceful and calm while she slept. He also liked to watch her sleep for a while before going to sleep himself. He didn't want to sound creepy but she was cute when she slept. She would sometimes mumble things in her sleep and there had been a few times he had heard his name. It made his heart soar when he thought of her dreaming of him. He had dreams about her sometimes so it was nice to know that he wasn't the only one. He had also heard her say I love you in her sleep and he could only assume she had been saying it to him. He already knew that she loved him. No one would be crazy enough to stick around through gunfights and kidnappings without loving the other person.

"Shh, go back to sleep," he whispered as her eyes slowly started to open. They looked glazed over as she tried to focus on him. She was clearly still half asleep as she continued to blink a number of times so her eyes could finally see properly.

She lifted her head slowly to meet his eyes. Hers were still slightly closed as she looked at him.

"Hmm," she said as she leaned into him and kissed him. Her lips were soft and gentle as they pressed against his. He pulled her closer to him as he deepened the kiss, tasting her as he pushed her mouth open with his tongue. Their bodies were pressed together, skin against skin as they wrapped themselves around each other. Sage gently pushed Mia onto her back as he bent over her and kissed her while he laid on his side.

Mia wrapped her arms around his neck as she intertwined her fingers in his hair. The need and want for each other grew as their tongues grazed teeth and lips. Sage soon traced a line of kisses down her neck while Mia moaned. Sage only had a pair of comfy pants on and Mia had one of his t-shirts on. He tugged at his as he reached under the shirt, wanting to feel her body with his hands. Soon they were naked, skin on skin as they moved with each other under the covers. Their bodies touched and burned, almost as if the heat they felt within themselves had set their surroundings on fire.

Sage kissed and sucked at her skin, tasting her and feeling her as he ran his hands all over her body. She was beautiful, every curve of her body had been shaped so perfectly, from the dip of her hips to the backs of her knees. Every part of her sent a shiver of love and longing deep inside Sage's core. He would never get over the feeling she brought to him, he would never get over the color she had brought too as if she had turned on a light that had died so long ago. He loved Mia with every fiber of his being. It was a different love from the love he had for Laura; this love was deeper, stronger. He felt it was because she had stuck by him through everything and Laura he felt wouldn't have done anything like that.

He grazed his lips against her skin, fumbling as they moved, Mia reaching for him with her greedy hands and he couldn't stop himself from giving in to her completely. He reached across to his bedside table for the second time that day and pulled out another condom, grateful that he had thought about restocking his stash only days before. Their bodies rocked in time to each other as he placed himself between her legs again, wanting nothing more than to be inside her once more. He dipped his hips to meet hers as she moved hers up and into him, needing to be connected with him as soon as she possibly could. The desire that burned inside them both set them on fire as they became one and as they came apart together, Sage whispered the words he had been dying to say.

"I love you, Mia," he said as she moaned with pleasure.

He wasn't sure if she had heard him but that didn't

matter so much to him. The only thing that mattered was the fact that he had finally said the words that had been burning in his mouth for days. They had been on the tip of his tongue for the longest time and he was relieved he could finally share them and know for sure that he meant them. He had held them in, wanting to make sure that when he did finally say those words, they were completely true and that there was nothing holding him back. There was nothing in his life that he wanted more than a future with Mia and because of how strongly he felt about that, he would stop at nothing until Laura, or whatever her real name was, was completely out of their lives. He didn't want to wait any longer to start the rest of his life with Mia. He had already pushed it aside for so long and there was no reason for him to do that anymore. Their relationship was stronger than ever and he was 100 percent ready to plan further into his life with her. He had tried his hardest to push her away and he didn't want that to ever happen again.

11

Mia felt a little bad for not saying anything back to Sage, especially considering she felt the same way but she was too scared and also extremely taken aback. She hadn't expected him to say it in the first place after all he hadn't been expressive with her when it came to actual words. He had of course shown her how much she meant to him by getting a tattoo that symbolized her but she hadn't heard him say the L word before. The other reason she hadn't said it was because she was terrified of him leaving her in the end. She didn't want to make herself so vulnerable in case he walked away with Laura which Mia really hoped wouldn't happen.

She had had the words on the tip of her tongue for the longest time but wasn't sure she was ready to say them back. There were so many things she needed to talk to Sage about first. She needed to make sure that everything would be okay in the end. Only after that would she say it back.

She loved Sage, loved him more than she had ever loved before and losing him would crush her but she had to try and stay strong. She didn't want her feelings for him to mess with his head because even though she didn't want to be without him, she would always want him to be happy, even if that meant she would be without him. She would make that sacrifice for him. The thought killed her, it made her want to curl up in a ball and cry but as Sage fell back to sleep beside her she rested her head against his chest and listened to his heartbeat. It didn't take long for Mia to fall back to sleep. She repeated Sage's last words in her head over and over again.

Mia looked around and realized she was standing in a dark hallway, a light in the distance flickered next to a closed door. She felt as if it was a sign that she was supposed to go to it. She wasn't sure exactly where she was as nothing looked familiar to her but nevertheless, she walked forward as she felt drawn to the light as if it were a beacon of hope, a lighthouse that was bringing her back to the shore.

She walked slowly toward the door, the floor creaking underneath her feet. Something felt wrong the further she walked forward but when she tried to turn back, a force took over her body and pushed her to continue. There was no going back. She had no other choice but to open the door as she arrived in front of it.

Her body shook as she stood still for a moment. Her heart raced and she could feel it in her chest. Sweat had started to form across her forehead and she could feel it as it dripped down the nape of her neck.

She lifted her hand and pulled the handle down, the metal cold against her skin.

She nudged the door open and let it swing until it stopped, revealing to her what was inside.

Shock filled her body as she saw Sage lying on a hospital bed, tubes and drips attached to him.

She noticed that one side of his face was covered as if he had injured his head. Mia walked slowly over to him as her heart calmed at the sight of Sage and although she was grateful there was nothing terrifying in front of her, she still didn't understand the scene she was taking in.

"Sage, what happened?" she asked, her voice soft and filled with concern as she reached out to take his hand in hers.

Sage looked at her with a confused expression on his face.

"Who are you?" he said as he pulled his hand away from her. The sting of rejection was strong in Mia's chest. How could he not know who she was? She couldn't understand what was going on. None of it made any sense to her as she searched his eyes for any form of recognition. There wasn't any. The man she loved continued to stare at her as if she were an alien that had landed before him.

"Sage, it's me, Mia," she replied. Tears started to well in her eyes. Her heart broke in her chest. There was no hope for her to recover from the pain that ripped through her body.

"I don't know who you are," he said, "get away from me."

Mia pulled back. The tears had already worked their way down her cheeks as her heart shattered in her chest. Movement caught her eye, it was coming from the corner of the room and as she turned to see what it was, a cry of pain escaped her lips. Her hand reached up and covered her mouth as the tears continued to fall.

Laura walked over to the other side of Sage's bed and took his hand in hers. He didn't recoil from her, instead, his entire face lit up and a smile spread across his lips.

"I think it's best you leave," Laura said as she looked at Mia. Her voice was sharp and stern, leaving no room for argument. Mia turned back to the door and as she turned away from them she noticed the tattoo of the lioness had gone and it became clear that Sage no longer knew her and he no longer wanted her either.

Mia woke up, her face wet with tears as the dream filled her head. She brought her hands to her face to wipe them away before Sage could see them as he was still sleeping next to her. She knew it was just a dream and she knew it had nothing to do with the present. She could remember seeing a picture of Sage in the hospital right after his accident when she had been doing research on Laura and so she also knew that because she felt threatened by Laura, her mind had played out the worst scenario ever, a life where Sage didn't even know who she was. It was a terrible thought, possibly even worse than him leaving her. Sage could be the best thing that had ever happened to her and she had no intention of losing him. She would fight for him if she had to.

Nothing has happened yet so you need to calm down, she said to herself.

She knew stressing about it would only cause her more pain but at the same time she had never had anything so real before and she was terrified of losing that.

"Good morning," Sage said from beside her. She looked over at him and her heart swelled with love as she took in his sleepy face.

"And to you," she replied, her voice filled with emotion. The dream was still strong in her mind and she tried not to let it get to her.

"What's wrong?" Sage asked. He sat up beside her and stroked her arm.

"Oh nothing, just a bad dream," she replied. "Are you hungry?"

She could see the concerned look on Sage's face and was relieved when he decided not to push the topic.

"Starving," he said as he licked his lips.

"Perfect, I think it's breakfast time," she replied as she got out of bed and started to head for the kitchen. She didn't want Sage to look at her face for too long. She knew her face always got a little splotchy whenever she cried and she didn't want Sage to know.

She decided to cook a full-blown breakfast as she took out eggs, bacon, bread, mushrooms, cheese, and tomatoes along with a few frying pans and spatulas. They hadn't been eating properly and she didn't want that to happen any longer.

"Why don't you make us coffee while I get breakfast started?" she said to Sage as he stood in the doorway of the kitchen.

"Yes, ma'am," he replied as he walked over to the kettle and switched it on before grabbing two mugs and the coffee jar.

Mia turned back to the task at hand as she started to fry some bacon. Sage didn't bother her as she cooked. Instead, he left her to do it by herself which she was grateful for. She put all her focus on making breakfast as she pushed her dream from her mind.

Once she was done she plated everything up and they both sat at the table to eat. It was easy for her to let go of her dream as she and Sage talked over breakfast. Just being around him made everything feel alright in the world. She was grateful he didn't ask her if she had heard him when he had told her he loved her. She was still processing it and wanted everything to settle first before she told him that she, of course, loved him too.

"What are your plans for the day?" Sage asked as he shoveled eggs and bacon into his mouth.

"I think I'm going to go to the club, just to check in and see how things are," she replied. Deep down she just wanted to know if Laura or Lorraine or whatever her name was had been around recently but of course she wouldn't tell Sage that. There was also a part of her that just wanted to get out of the house. As much as she had enjoyed her time with Sage recently, she longed for a little time alone so she could process her feelings. It wasn't just about the woman coming unexpectedly into their lives anymore, it was also about Sage expressing himself. It was all too much for Mia.

"That sounds like a good idea," he said. Mia thought so too. She finished her breakfast before Sage and watched him as he reached for seconds.

"Would you mind cleaning up while I go shower?" she asked.

"Oh, yes. Of course," Sage replied.

"Thank you," she said as she got up and left.

Mia had a quick shower and washed off all the bad energy that hung around her. She knew her mind was playing tricks on her and she had to stop herself before it got any worse. Sage was still with her and she had to remind herself of that.

She got ready and said goodbye to Sage as she left the house. She was grateful for the car that Sage had gotten for them. She had started hating riding the bike or calling for a cab to fetch her. As she drove, she thought about what she would do if she saw Lorriane at the club. She thought that maybe she would hit her and curse her for ruining her perfect life but she knew she wouldn't do that. She wouldn't want to do anything that might cause Sage to hate her.

Mia sat in the car for a while once she arrived at the club. She tried to convince herself that no matter what happened once she walked through the doors, every-thing would still be okay. After a few moments, she stepped out of the car and walked over to the doors. She took a deep breath and proceeded to walk in. After scanning the room she was relieved to notice that Lorraine wasn't there so she made her way over to the Hell Kats who stood at the bar.

"Hey ladies, how's it going?" she asked. They were all happy to see her as they took their turns to hug her. At that moment, Mia was grateful for their support and friendship. If all else failed, she knew she could always count on them.

"Mia, it's so good to see you. Nothing exciting has happened recently," one said in answer to her question. She wasn't sure if they would know that she wanted to know specifically about Lorraine without having to ask but she knew that if she wanted answers she would have to ask the one question she was dying to have answered.

"Oh, that's great. Has...um...has Lorraine or Laura or whatever name she goes by been around recently?" she asked. She was nervous to ask but there was no point in beating around the bush either.

They all shook their heads at the same time.

"No, she hasn't. It's been rather quiet without her drunk ramblings," one of the girls said.

Although it was music to Mia's ears, she had a bad feeling. It didn't make sense that she had practically forced her presence on everyone and then disappeared. Warning bells went off in her head as the thought crossed her mind. She didn't want to alarm the girls though so she made out as if it was good news.

"That's great news. I really hope our last interaction with her was the last one we'll ever have," she replied.

She wasn't 100 percent sure if it would be the last time they saw her but a girl could dream, right?

She sat down with the girls and chatted about a few things, trying to distract herself as much as she could. She wanted to really enjoy the time she had away from the house even though Sage's words were still on repeat in the back of her mind. It was a dream come true that Sage felt that way about her. She had longed for it for so long but she felt that it had happened at the wrong time. Everything was extremely messed up and she needed that to be sorted first. She thought that maybe Sage had only said it because he felt like he had to reassure her instead of actually meaning it. The thought of him saying it just to put her mind at ease scared her because he could easily take it back, although she believed Sage wasn't the type of person to say something he didn't mean. Mia hated herself for overthinking it so much when she should, in fact, be happy about it.

Mia's phone went off mid-thought and when she looked at the screen, she saw Sage's name flashing.

"Hey, Sage," she said. She wasn't sure why he would be calling her and her mind went crazy at the possible reasons.

"Hey, Mia. I'm sorry to bother you but you need to come back to the house," he replied. His voice was filled with concern and worry.

"What's happened?" Mia asked as the worst thoughts came to mind.

"Nothing has actually happened but I've got some news and to be honest, it doesn't sound good," he said. She knew he wouldn't tell her anything over the phone. It sounded serious.

"Okay, I'm leaving now," she said as she wordlessly waved goodbye to the Hell Kats and walked out of the doors.

Whatever had happened since she left was more important than staying at the club.

12

Sage sat in his office with his head between his hands. He was struggling emotionally after the phone call he had had with Laura's parents. As he had thought, Laura had not returned from Afghanistan after the bombing nor had they heard of any other news about her. For her family, she had died and that was it, case closed. Sage found it extremely unfair how someone could claim to be someone who wasn't alive. Causing people to remember the pain of losing them in the process was just cruel. He wanted to make Lorriane pay for what she'd done. It was disgusting and inhumane. When Sage had been talking to Laura's parents, he could hear the pain in their voices as they spoke about their daughter. He couldn't imagine the pain they had gone through when they lost her, no parent should live through losing a child.

A part of him wished he could go back in time and change how everything had played out. He would've tried harder to convince Laura not to go on the mission. It would've been the only way for him to save her considering he couldn't save her from the bombing. There had been times when he had thought he could've gotten to her sooner when the bomb went off but he also knew that wouldn't have worked either; she was too far away from him. He didn't know how things would've worked out between them but at least she still would've been alive.

His mind traveled back to his conversation as he waited for Mia to arrive back at the house.

"Hi, am I speaking to Mr. Johnson?" Sage asked when someone had picked up.

"Yes, this is him. How may I help?"

It was clear he hadn't recognized Sage's voice. He wasn't surprised though as he hadn't spoken to them since the funeral.

"Mr. Johnson... I don't know if you remember me but my name is Sage," he said. He wanted to make sure that Laura's father was comfortable talking to him first before he jumped into asking any questions. It was hard enough just having to think about the fact that he would have to bring up something so painful.

"There's only one Sage I know of. After all, that's a very unique name. It's been a while, son, how have you been?" he

asked through the phone. Sage's heart ached when he called him 'son'. He couldn't bear breaking their hearts.

"I'm doing well thanks, sir, and how are you?" Sage replied. He felt like it was a very stupid question to ask because after two years they probably still felt the same pain as the day they had found out about the incident.

"Oh, we're doing alright considering the circumstances," he said.

Sage felt sorry for the Johnsons. He had lost someone he loved but for him, he had managed to move on. For them, it would be not as easy as that. Sage could remember the day of the funeral and how heartbroken Laura's parents had been. Seeing them sobbing was engraved in his mind. He had tried to forget that day ever since it had happened as it had been extremely hard for him too.

"I'm glad to hear that, sir," Sage replied. He wasn't sure how he could get to the point without it coming out unkind. He really didn't want to cause any pain.

"Well, Sage, I'm sure you haven't called just to find out how we are. So what can I do for you?" He was relieved that he had cut to the chase without Sage having to do it. He still had no idea how to ask such hard questions.

"You see, sir, I've had a run-in with a woman and sadly she is claiming to be Laura..." Sage finally said. He didn't see the point in dragging it out any longer than necessary. His heart was pounding in his ears as the silence dragged on from the other side of the phone.

"Sir, are you still there?" he said worried that he had fainted with shock.

"Yes, yes, I'm still here..." he replied, "I honestly don't know what to say other than it's impossible that Laura could be alive."

Sage already knew that but was glad to hear that he wasn't the only one who thought that. It was a relief to him that he could finally hear that Lorraine was not Laura, but the question that sprung to his mind was if it wasn't Laura then why claim to be her?

He had his suspicions that something bigger was happening but he still didn't know what.

"I'm so sorry to have brought this up, I know it can't be easy," Sage said.

"I'm truly shocked to hear that someone is claiming to be my daughter. I just don't understand it," he replied. Sage could hear the muted pain in his voice, it was heartbreaking.

"I'm trying to figure that out, sir. I thought it could be a female family relative? Is there anyone you could think of that would do something like this?" Sage asked. He wanted to rule out any options of it being a family member before doing anything to stop the woman.

"Well, I know for sure it isn't her sister. She lives very close to us and visits us at least twice a week and when it comes to other female relatives, well, she doesn't have any female cousins that would be around her age or any female cousins in general," Mr. Johnson said. The rage in Sage's chest grew as he *got the answers he needed. He could kill the Lorraine woman for bringing up the past he had worked so hard to forget. It wasn't that he wanted to forget Laura completely but he needed to move on with his life.*

"I'm going to get to the bottom of this, sir, and whoever could be so cruel is going to pay for what they've done. I am so sorry for bringing up so many painful memories," Sage said.

"We'll be alright, son. We know that our sweet angel is resting peacefully but I truly hope you're happy. We know it was hard on you too."

Sage didn't want to think about how much pain he had gone through, he didn't want to live through it again.

"Thank you, sir. Thank you so much for giving me your time. I'll be getting to the bottom of this mess as quickly as possible," Sage replied.

"Take care, son, we wish you all the best," Mr. Johnson said before he ended the call.

It was hard for him to hear him be so kind. He didn't feel as if he deserved that amount of kindness after not saving their daughter. He knew it wasn't his fault and he knew they knew that too but he wouldn't have held it against them if they blamed him partly.

When he had called Mia to go back to the house, he could hear that she was worried and he hoped she didn't think it was because he was leaving. He had noticed how she had been acting recently and he knew she was scared but he had no intention of leaving her. The thought hadn't even crossed his mind. He could understand why she was scared. It would have been hard for him too if the roles had been reversed. He hated the thought of someone taking Mia from him.

He was hoping that Mia would have told him she loved him too when they had woken up but he still wasn't sure if she had heard him. She didn't act too weirdly toward him during breakfast but she did hurry out of the house rather quickly. He just wanted everything to go back to how it had been before all the drama had started. Everything had been going so well between them. He could hear the front door being opened as he brought his mind back to the present. He had to share the news with Mia so they could work out what to do next. He listened as Mia's footsteps started to get louder the closer she got to his office. He was excited to see her again even though it had only been a few hours since she had left.

"Hey," she said as she walked into his office. He could see she was a bit nervous as she sat down in the chair opposite him.

"Hey, how's the club looking?" he asked. He wanted to make her feel relaxed.

"Everything is going well, nothing out of the ordinary has happened recently," she replied. Sage could see her getting a little more comfortable as she noticed his energy was calm.

"That's good, that's very good," Sage said.

"So, what's the news you have to tell me?" she asked.

"Well, I phoned Laura's parents today and what they told me was very interesting," he said. He could see Mia's interest piqued at the mention of Laura.

"What did they say, do they know if she's alive?" she asked. Her voice filled with intrigue.

"She's not alive. She died two years ago and that's it. They said her sister visits them often so it can't be her and she doesn't have any cousins who could be pretending to be her either," he said. He watched as the expression on Mia's face became serious.

"What does this mean then?" she asked.

Sage didn't actually know what it meant, all he knew was that someone had to stop Lorraine before someone got hurt.

"I honestly don't know what we're going to do. I really need to figure exactly what's going on," he replied.

"Do you think it could have something to do with the Omens?" Mia asked.

Sage had thought that they could be involved, the act of pretending to be someone else seemed cruel enough that the Omens could be behind it.

"I suspect it could have something to do with them, I just don't know what their angle is," he said.

The first thought Sage had was to just go looking for the Omens, taking them by surprise but he knew better than that. He had learned his lesson the first time that the Omens should be taken seriously.

"I think we should prepare ourselves for whatever could be coming our way. All of this sounds too dangerous for my liking," Mia said.

Sage was proud of Mia. She had grown so much since she had moved to Florida and it showed when they were in trouble. Her face was strong and serious as if she was already prepared mentally for whatever was going to happen.

"I believe you're right, we have to stand strong against this," he replied. He wished he could keep Mia out of it. It hurt him to think that he could lose yet another woman during a fight he had no control over. He knew she wouldn't stay out of it.

He could see that Mia was about to respond just as the sound of his computer went off, notifying him that he had received an email.

"Hold that thought," he said as he turned to his computer to look at the email. He saw Fiona's name and knew immediately that it was important. He scanned through the email, his eyebrows raised as his thoughts became real.

"What does it say?" Mia asked from in front of him.

Sage proceeded to read the email out loud.

'Sage, Lorraine has grown up in Florida all her life so there is no way she could be Laura. Her DNA is also proof of that. She ties back to the Omens and is a threat to us. You need to be on high alert.'

The message was short and to the point. It set off warning bells in Sage's mind as he read it over again in his head. His suspicions had been right and it was clear that the Omens would stop at nothing until they brought down the Screaming Demons. Sage knew he wouldn't go down without a fight.

"Shit, this isn't good, Sage," Mia said after listening to the email and Sage had to agree. Whenever the Omens were involved, it only meant trouble.

"I'm going to call Fiona and see what she wants us to do," he replied as he reached for the phone that lay on his desk. Fiona picked up almost immediately.

"Hi, Fiona. Let me put you on loudspeaker because Mia is with me," he said as he quickly pressed the loudspeaker icon on his phone. "Go ahead, Fiona."

"Hi, guys. Listen, whatever the Omens have planned is definitely not going to be good for us. I think it's best if I send more guys to you," Fiona said, her voice strong and powerful.

Sage knew it was the best idea for them. They couldn't risk anything happening and they would definitely need more help if the Omens were playing tricks.

"That would help a lot, thank you, Fiona," Mia said.

"Yes, that would definitely be good for us," Sage agreed.

"Okay, perfect. They'll arrive by tomorrow. In the meantime, stay alert at all times. Anything could happen and we have to be prepared," Fiona said.

"Of course," Sage replied.

"Good, I've gotta go. I need to pick out the best men for this. Let me know if anything happens," Fiona said just before the line went dead. Sage knew that if Fiona felt they needed back up there could only be one way things could go and it became a little frightening for him. He had been trained to survive at all costs and he could handle tough situations but he also knew that they were completely blindsided by what could happen. He hoped that they would make it out alive because what-ever the Omens had planned had to be big. It would explain the lengths they had gone to just to try to catch them by surprise.

Sage looked at Mia as the severity of the situation sunk in. Whatever was going to happen sounded big and there was no way they could really know what the Omens had planned until they attacked. He knew he would protect Mia no matter what happened. In the end, her life meant everything to him. He couldn't risk losing her after he had just let her into his heart. He loved her more than he had loved anyone before and that was huge for him. He didn't want to picture his life without her because for the first time in the longest time he could picture himself settling down with someone. He had tried to cut himself off from that. Even when he had met Laura he had tried to stay away from her because of the type of job they had. He loved to play the protector, no matter what the situation was.

13

Mia slept a lot better after Fiona had said she'd send more men to them for back up. There was a heavy feeling in her chest about what the Omens could be up to and she knew they would need all the help they could get, especially considering what had happened the last time they had made their presence known. She tried not to think back to the days when she was taken or when Sage had been trapped. The image of being tortured by the Omens still haunted her. The days when Sage had been gone always came back to her mind when she let herself get too emotional, and she didn't want the Omens to get the best of her. The Omens were definitely cruel and heartless people who clearly didn't have any empathy for others which made Mia sick to her stomach. For the first time in a long time, Mia cuddled up next to Sage as they fell asleep together, completely content.

Neither of them had any dreams that night; they had no doubt in their minds that everything would work out in the end and for once they rested easy.

Mia woke up the next day without any memory of having had a bad dream which she was grateful for. She felt that no matter what happened she was ready and would take down anyone who would do anything to try to hurt her. She had proved to herself time and time again that she was a lot stronger than she had ever expected and she knew that in the face of her enemies she would fight until her last breath. Sage shifted beside her as she moved to draw him closer to her, his body warm and comforting next to hers.

"Good morning," Sage said half asleep.

"Did I wake you?" she asked. She had tried to be as gentle as possible when she moved.

"No, no, I've been on the verge of waking up for a while," he replied as he stretched. The atmosphere around them felt lighter than it had for a while and although they were still concerned about the Omens, they felt more positive about the situation.

"Why don't you stay in bed while I make us some breakfast?" Sage asked. Even though Mia loved cooking, she appreciated him making the effort for her.

"That sounds wonderful," she replied. She watched

Sage get up and leave while she snuggled further into the bed. She knew she would have to get up eventually but she decided she would enjoy the moment while it lasted. She could hear Sage in the kitchen and decided to have a shower while she waited. There wasn't much time for them to waste before the new arrivals would arrive and she wanted to be at the club for when they got there. As she got out of the shower, Mia could hear Sage whistling as he walked down the hallway and back into the room.

"Mia?" he called from the bedroom.

"I'm just getting out of the shower, I'll be out in a minute," she called back.

She looked at herself in the mirror and noticed that although she felt different, she didn't look very different. She felt as if the growth she had gone through should show more on the outside because she wasn't the same person she had been months before. Her life had gone from one extreme to the next and she wasn't sure which one was better. She loved her life but she was unsure of what to do next. There was going to be a war and she knew that but what would happen after that was so unknown it scared her.

She dried herself off and wrapped her bathrobe around her as she entered the bedroom again. Mia was welcomed by a delicious scent of food as she saw Sage had sat down on the bed with a tray that had a huge pile of pancakes stacked on a plate with maple syrup and coffee. She couldn't help but smile as she took it all in. He had gone further than she had thought he would and he had done it all for her.

He smiled at her as she placed herself on the bed across from him. She reached over and picked up the cup of coffee that she knew was hers because it had milk in it while Sage liked his coffee black.

"While you were in the shower I received a message from Adam. Apparently, the guys from Pine Hill have arrived and want to meet at the club," Sage said.

"We should probably go soon then, shouldn't we?" she asked as she placed a few pancakes on her plate and cut into them.

"We can go after breakfast. It sounds like they want a huge party and its not even noon yet!" he exclaimed. Mia wanted to laugh at Sage's reaction and it was so easy for her to remember why she loved him. It wasn't about his looks or anything like that. It was about who he was as a person. She almost felt compelled to tell him that she loved him but she held herself back, still unsure about the future. Once they had both eaten enough, Sage went and showered quickly before they made their way to the bar.

"What do you think could happen with the Omens?" Mia asked as Sage drove them to the bar. She turned to look at his face as his eyes stayed glued to the road.

"I honestly don't know. I can't seem to think what they could be up to, especially considering they involved Laura's name. None of it makes any sense and that scares me the most," he replied. Mia could tell that he was being genuine about his feelings and although it scared her a little, she could respect the fact that he wasn't trying to sugarcoat the situation for her. They all knew something big would happen.

"At least we've got some back up now," she said with a small smile. Sage smiled back at her in return.

"I'm hoping we won't need it but anything is possible at this rate," he said and even as he said it Mia knew that they'd probably need the back up because she had had a bad feeling in her chest for days. They drove in silence the rest of the way to the club and as they got closer they both got nervous about what lay ahead of them but once they arrived at the club Mia felt that being with the new recruits would help relax both her and Sage.

When they walked through the doors, they were welcomed by all the Screaming Demons and the party was already well underway. Mia decided to join in on the fun but decided not to drink at the same time. She felt it would be a good way to get to know all the new recruits and make them feel welcomed. Sage soon joined in and danced with Mia. For the first time in a long time, they were having fun and for a while, they were both distracted from the trouble that could be happening very soon. The room was filled with laughing and joking and everyone was dancing. It feels good to laugh again, Mia thought. Sage wrapped his arms around Mia as they danced. He pulled her close to him protectively and she rested her head against his chest listening to his heartbeat as they danced. They felt as if they were wrapped up in their own little world for a while, away from all the drama where it was just the two of them. It felt good and they wished it could stay that way. Mia could see Adam from the corner of her eye and noticed he didn't look as happy as everyone else.

"Something's up with Adam," she whispered to Sage as they continued to dance. Sage looked around the room until his eyes landed on Adam who stood still against the bar as he watched the crowd dance around him.

"Let's go talk to him," he said as he took her hand and led her over to Adam. She followed willingly.

"Hey, Adam," Sage said as they got to him. He looked at them with a small smile.

"Hey, guys. There's quite a crowd today," he replied as he looked around the room. Both Sage and Mia nodded their heads in agreement.

"One big happy family," Mia said. She noticed the worried look on Adam's face and started to feel a little uneasy.

"Adam, what's going on? You don't look so happy

today," Sage asked. It was clear he had picked up on Adam's expression.

"It's the Omens. They have 23 people and they're coming for us, man. I've received news that they were the ones who contacted the law enforcement officers and they haven't stopped. Yes, they've been off of our backs but they know everything," Adam said.

Mia didn't like what she heard. It didn't sound good for the Screaming Demons at all.

"What do you think we should do about this?" Sage asked. The party around them was still going and no one was paying attention to their conversation.

"Honestly, I think we need to shut it down. Everything. There's only one way this could go and I'm not liking our odds," he replied. Mia knew he was right but shutting everything down was a big step to take. She looked around at all the friends she had made, all the people who she considered to be family. They were all so happy and she wished it could stay that way.

"I agree with Adam," she said.

If law enforcement was hot on their tracks there could only be one solution. They would have to get rid of everything and that meant more than just shutting it down. They couldn't risk anyone finding out what they did behind the scenes. No one needed to know about the drugs and the people they were involved with. That had to stay between them.

"Okay, let's shut down the party and I think it's best if we get rid of any evidence we have here," Sage replied. The three of them looked at each other and nodded their heads in agreement.

"Listen up!!" Sage shouted while Adam started to walk to the office. Everyone stopped and someone turned down the music. "Unfortunately, we're going to have to shut down the party ladies and gents," he continued. The crowd made a noise in disagreement but no one fought back. It was clear they all knew something was up. Sage had enough authority over the club that people trusted his instincts.

"We need all ears to the ground right now. The Omens are coming and we need to be prepared. I need a few guys to go help Adam in the office. We're shutting it down and getting rid of everything!" he said. A few men stepped forward and Sage indicated for them to go to Adam. Mia watched as Sage took control, ordering people to do certain things and making sure everything was sorted.

She couldn't help but find it extremely sexy watching him as he took charge. She knew at that moment that there were bigger things to worry about but her heart beamed with pride as she watched the true leader Sage was. Sage made his way to her after giving orders to the men.

"I need to call Fiona and tell her what's going on," he said.

"You're right, she'd want to know. We need to know what our next move is," she replied. Fiona, of course, would have to agree with them. They had no other choice but to get rid of everything that could tie them to any of the shady business they had done.

Sage walked away from Mia as he dialed Fiona's number and after a few minutes he was back at her side.

"What did Fiona say?" Mia asked.

"She agreed that we need to shut everything down. She even suggested that we burn everything to the ground if needed," he replied. She was glad Fiona agreed with Sage as it was already too late to turn back as Adam had already started to rip up all the folders in the office.

"Do you think that's necessary?" she asked. It seemed a bit extreme to her when she thought about it.

"Honestly, I don't think we need to burn it all down but maybe we should burn all the evidence. That way there'll definitely be nothing for anyone to find," he said.

"I agree. Maybe tell Adam and the guys to do that. I would hate to lose this place," she said as she looked around the bar. It held so many memories for her and she didn't want to burn it to the ground because of the Omens, especially not because of them. Sage went over to Adam and Mia watched as Adam nodded along to what Sage was saying. At least everyone is on the same page, she thought.

Mia realized how tired she was as she looked over at the clock. It was still early but she longed to be at home, away from all the noise and chaos if only for a while. She knew the situation wouldn't just go away after sleeping. It would still be there when she woke up but a part of her just wanted it to be done. She was tired of it all and she wished she had a more normal life. She looked over at Sage and knew that she would go anywhere he went. She would follow him regardless of the situation, which is why she hadn't walked away already. She knew she could've walked away when he had been kidnapped. She could have found him and then left for good. Maybe she could've been a famous artist somewhere but she also knew that her life would've been empty without Sage by her side.

Sage made his way back to her and she felt comfortable with him by her side. She knew at that moment that she had made the right choice by wanting to stay with the Screaming Demons. Even if it was filled with drama and near-death experiences, she would take it in a heartbeat over any other life she could've had. Sage took her hand and led her toward the door.

"Let's go home," he said. Mia nodded her head and followed him as he led her to the car. She loved him with all that she had and there would be no way she would leave him. She knew he had chosen her and her heart finally relaxed after all the worry of him leaving. Lorraine was no longer a threat to their relationship. She was still a threat but a threat they could fight together.

14

They made their way home in silence while they both thought about the Omens. They knew that they had to do something but there was no chance of them running. It was too late for that. It was clear that the Omens wouldn't stop until the Screaming Demons paid for what they had done to their ringleader. It was frustrating to think that they couldn't just let the past go.

"Don't you think it's pathetic that this is all over their stupid ringleader?" Mia asked as they parked in the driveway.

"I think it has something to do with you too. I mean if you hadn't turned on them in the first place, none of this would've happened," he replied.

"I suppose you're right," she said. The Omens would

have to be completely shut down for them to ever have a normal life together and it was scary to think that way.

It was only 3 pm when Sage and Mia arrived home after the little party at the bar. Sage was a little on edge because of the news from Adam. He still couldn't believe that they had to burn all the folders and then also wipe all the hard drives clean so nothing could be traced back to anyone in the Screaming Demons. He wasn't sure what would happen next but he had a feeling in his chest that he would find out soon enough. It seemed as if the Omens were just about ready to attack and Sage had started to get a little worried. Of course, he could handle whatever was thrown his way but there was a huge part of him that wanted all the drama to end. He wasn't sure how much longer he could go on living in constant fear of something happening to him or to Mia. He honestly didn't want to constantly put Mia in danger.

"What are you thinking about?" Mia asked as they entered the house. He looked at Mia and saw how worried she looked. He wasn't sure if she was worried about him or just worried in general. Sage wished for a distraction for the rest of the evening; he didn't want to spend too much time thinking negatively and he also needed to stay focused because if he got too emotional before anything actually happened, he might not be able to protect either of them properly. The next steps would be vital in the grander scheme of things. If either of them messed up, it could all be over and not for the Omens but for them.

"I'm just thinking of what could be the Omens' next move. They've literally taken us by surprise so far and I can't for the life of me figure out what's happening. The thing I don't understand is why they've ratted us out to law enforcement and then tried to trick me into believing Laura wasn't dead. Why?" he asked. He didn't want to worry Mia but he had found that he felt better when they talked things through, especially when he was a bit confused.

"I've been thinking the same thing and I'm also confused as to why they haven't attacked yet, like what's the plan you know?" Mia wondered.

Sage really enjoyed the fact that he and Mia had grown so much together that it meant they could talk openly about almost anything. He wondered if she loved him considering she still hadn't said it back but a part of him knew that she did. He could tell by the way she looked at him and for him, that was enough.

"I feel as if we should be prepared for just about anything. I don't know what their next move will be but I can only assume it's going to be big," Sage replied. He wished that they could leave so they could be as far away from the Omens as possible but he also knew that they wouldn't stop looking for them, they wouldn't walk away until someone was dead.

"Well let's try and enjoy the rest of the day, shall we?' Mia suggested. Sage appreciated Mia's idea but also knew that he wouldn't be able to stop thinking about the Omens, not until they made their next move.

Sage watched as Mia made her way to the kitchen and started to prepare them some lunch and within no time they were at the dining room table eating. They both felt a little more relaxed, grateful that they had this house that they shared together. As he watched her from across the table, Sage realized that he wanted to be with Mia for the rest of his life and not just as boyfriend and girlfriend; he knew he wanted to marry her. It shocked him as the thought went around in his mind. He knew he cared for and loved her but he never thought he'd be ready to think of marriage again. It brought a smile to his lips as he realized how much he liked the idea.

"What are you smiling about?" Mia asked.

"Oh, nothing. Just really enjoying the lunch you made," he replied. She eyed him suspiciously as she took a bite of the chicken and mayo sandwich she made. He knew he would have to wait for the right moment to ask her to marry him and their current situation was definitely not it.

Once they were finished with their lunch, they made

their way to the lounge. They were both ready to just relax for the rest of the day. They both needed a bit of a break from everything and because they had to stick around, they would have to settle for staying at the house. It wasn't too bad considering they got to be around each other. The toll of everything weighed heavily on their shoulders and within 30 minutes of the movie they put on, they were both fast asleep on the couch.

Sage woke up a few hours later and found the house covered in darkness. He could hear Mia breathing softly next to him while she continued to sleep. He looked at the digital clock that beamed in the corner of the room and saw it was almost 9 pm. He had slept solidly, without any dreams again as he had blacked out completely. He couldn't believe that they had slept for so long. He was about to get up and switch on the lights when he heard someone yelling from outside the house. He sat still for a moment so he could listen, It didn't take him long to figure out who it was.

"Sage, come out, come out wherever you are!" the person yelled. He recognized the voice as Lorraine and he knew the next part of the Omens plan had begun.

"Mia, wake up," he whispered. He wanted to look outside to see exactly what was going on but he also didn't want to leave Mia defenseless while asleep. She woke up a little shocked as he shook her gently.

"Sage, what's going on?" she asked as she noticed the yelling that had started to get louder from outside.

"They're here, Lorraine is here and I don't think she's alone but I want to peek through the window to see what we're dealing with," Sage replied as he got up off of the couch and walked toward the nearest window. Mia followed close behind him. Neither of them turned any of the lights on. Sage gently pulled back one of the curtains and peeked through. He tried to make his movements a little as possible so he wouldn't be seen. He knew that there was no way out of the house but maybe if they kept quiet, Lorraine would leave.

He could make out eleven figures, one being Lorraine. It was two against eleven which meant defeat. His heart sank as he realized that they were trapped.

"We know you're in there! We've been watching you for a while, Sage," Lorraine shouted. Mia and Sage looked at each other. Neither of them knew what to do, there was nowhere for them to hide. They watched quietly as Lorraine and her men made their way toward the house. They heard a stone go through the window as they started breaking into the house. Sage grabbed Mia and pulled her away from the windows so she wouldn't get cut by any broken glass.

"What are we going to do?" she asked. Sage could hear the worry in her voice. He knew that there was nothing he could do but fight when they eventually made it into the house. He made a run for his office to get one of his guns.

"Shouldn't I have one too?" Mia asked when he returned. He considered getting one for her but decided against it. He knew she didn't have much experience when it came to guns and he didn't want to risk her falling short if a fight broke out which he knew was inevitable.

"Just stay with me and you'll be fine," he replied. He knew he'd throw himself in front of bullets for her if it came to it. It dawned on him that it could be the end of the line for them both and he decided to do one last thing because he may never get the chance again. He turned to Mia and leaned into her, locking his lips with hers in one final kiss between the two of them.

"Just in case," he said as he pulled away from her. Mia looked shocked for a moment before she smiled at him gently.

"We'll get through this," she said. Sage loved her attitude and willed himself to believe her but it was hard to look on the positive side of the situation.

They heard laughing as Lorraine and her men made it into the house. It was clear that the Omens were enjoying themselves as they knocked furniture over and broke things on their way toward Sage and Mia. Sage's heartbeat sped up as he waited for them to get closer, he tightly gripped Mia's hand and pulled her slightly behind him. If they started shooting, he wanted her to be safe. Soon enough, Lorraine and her team were standing in front of them, guns in their hands as they scanned the room. Lorraine smiled sweetly as she stared at Sage.

"You know, all of this could've been avoided if you had just believed me," she said as she waved her gun in the air, emphasizing what she was talking about.

Sage felt sick to his stomach as he noticed that they all had guns. He knew that if they opened fire, it would be over almost instantly.

"What do you want, Lorraine?" Sage asked. He wasn't interested in prolonging the events that seemed to have been planned well in advance. He knew he should've made a better plan for himself and Mia but he didn't think everything would happen so quickly. He thought they still had time.

"Well, I wanted information but considering you didn't give it to me, there's nothing else to do but to get rid of you," she replied as she shrugged her shoulders. Her expression was passive and her voice was calm as she spoke. It was unnerving. She really was heartless, Sage thought.

Sage began to push Mia back and raised his gun as he moved. Every fiber in his body told him not to act so quickly but he couldn't help himself.

"Now, now, Sage, don't do something you'll regret," she said.

Sage didn't think twice as he ran, pulling Mia with him as he made his way to his office. Lorraine and her men followed close behind. A few shots were let loose as they ran from room to room trying to find somewhere to hide. They didn't have many options as the Omens followed them throughout the house, shooting and laughing as they went. It seemed to be a game to them and that upset Sage the most. It wasn't just his life on the line but it was also Mia's.

As Sage looked back, he could see that Lorraine was no longer with the men and there were only six of them behind them. He thought it would be the perfect chance to get out as he pulled Mia with him toward the back doors of the house.

"Come on, Mia, we have to go," he said as he ran through the doors not waiting for her to reply. He knew they could run out behind the house. He had placed a gate in the fence that led out to the woods behind their house and it was the only way they could lose the Omens. It was hugely disappointing to find that Lorraine had gone to the back of the house with the other four missing men. Obviously, she had suspected that they would try to escape through the back of the house. Sage was out of ideas as he faced defeat. He couldn't save Mia or himself.

"You've got to think ahead, Sage. You didn't honestly believe you would be getting out of this, did you?" Lorraine asked as she watched them. He wanted to attack her, shoot her right in the chest but he couldn't. They would be able to shoot him down quicker.

"So what's the plan, Lorraine?" Sage asked. He was curious if she would even answer his question. He wanted to stall, buy more time even though he had no other plan.

"Well, wouldn't you like to know, but it doesn't work that way. I guess you'll just have to find out," she said. Sage and Mia watched as the four men behind Lorraine separated, two went toward Sage and the other two went toward Mia. Quickly and forcefully they tied their hands up. One of the men took the gun out of Sage's hands while he was tied up. He didn't even have the chance to injure anyone in the process.

"Take them to their pantry, tie up their feet and lock the door behind you. The game has just started," Lorraine said. The men did as they were told and led Sage and Mia back into the house. They pushed them into the pantry and they both fell on to their asses. The men then tied them up by their feet and left, locking the door behind them.

"Shit, we're screwed, aren't we?" Mia asked. Sage didn't know how he would get them out of the mess they were in. His hands were tied tightly behind his back.

"BURN IT TO THE GROUND!" he suddenly heard Lorraine yell from somewhere outside of the house. Alarm bells went off in his head as he realized what she meant. Their plan was to burn the house down with them inside.

The thought of the house burning around them scared Sage and Mia. It amazed them how the Omens could be so cruel and do such a thing. It didn't surprise them but they just couldn't understand how anyone could do that to another person. Obviously, they shouldn't be too shocked considering it was the Omens but it just wasn't right.

"Do you think they'll wait outside for us to die?" Mia asked Sage. Her voice was shaky when she said the word die. The gravity of it sank in almost immediately. She knew they'd die long before the flames got to them.

"We're not going to die, Mia. I promised I'd look after you and that's what I intend to do," Sage replied. Mia knew that he meant well but it didn't take away from the fact that they were trapped in a burning house. He couldn't expect to be some sort of superhero all of a sudden. Not even she would expect him to be able to get out of there.

"What are we going to do?" she asked. Her voice was soft, almost a whisper. Her thoughts ran wild as she pictured the house crushing them as it burned to the ground. She had to admit that she had watched a lot of horror movies and TV series that had cases of houses burning with people trapped inside and it made her head hurt as all those images came to mind. She could picture paramedics arriving at the house and pulling their bones from the rubble. It almost made her sick.

Mia kept thinking about how her life hadn't even started yet, she hadn't even accomplished any of her dreams. She knew that when she had moved to Florida she had hoped for more and there had been a time when it seemed like that could happen but as they sat tied up in the pantry of their kitchen, Mia hated herself for not doing more. She hadn't gotten very far with her paint-ings. In fact, she still hadn't shown anyone her work and she also hadn't managed to really have any sort of future with Sage. Her mind traveled back to the last time she had seen her parents and she realized she probably wouldn't be able to make things right with them. All of her mistakes flashed before her as if she was watching her life from the very beginning.

Is this what it feels like to have your life flash before your eyes, she thought to herself. She couldn't stand reliving her life, even if it were just memories. She didn't want to think about all the mistakes she had made. She knew she had messed up a lot and there could be no way for her to change that and she knew that if she hadn't made those mistakes she wouldn't have found Sage.

Sage kept quiet next to her. He had no idea what they were going to do but he didn't want Mia to lose faith. He knew he would do whatever he could to get them out of there. Although she hadn't said much in a while, he could see that she was freaking out internally; it was written all over her face. He wanted to settle her but he didn't have much time to waste. Sooner or later the smoke would knock them out and then there would be no hope of getting out. He tried to think of ideas, anything that could work in their favor. He looked around the pantry and was disappointed when he didn't see any sort of weapon or knife they could use. He knew it was a long shot to hope for that but it was worth the thought.

Mia tried her hardest to keep calm even though words of panic tumbled out of her mouth. She didn't want Sage to know just how scared she was. Of course, she knew he would understand but she wanted to stay strong because she had no other choice. There was no way she could be weak in that situation especially because she could smell the smoke coming through the door. They were burning her house down while they were locked in it. She thought about all her paintings. She had never gotten around to showing Sage any of them and she wished she had. He would've been able to see how much she loved him just by looking at her paintings of him and her heart broke at the thought of them being burnt to nothing. She really wanted to cry as the seriousness of the situation sunk in. No one could save them, no one even knew they had been attacked. Mia wanted to say goodbye to Sage, she finally wanted to tell him that she loved him. Tears formed in her eyes as she looked over at Sage who had been muttering to himself since they had been locked up in the pantry.

"Sage, I just wanted to tell you that-," she began before Sage interrupted her.

"No, Mia, there will be no goodbyes or anything like that. We're going to get out of here and still live a long and happy life," he said.

She didn't want to think about the fact that she may never get the chance to spend the rest of her life with him. Just the thought of it made her want to scream in pain. She didn't care so much about losing the house. They could always rebuild it and create new memories but her mind went to the dark side of her thoughts as she realized that they might die. She tried to push the thoughts out of her mind but it was hard to think straight as the smoke had slowly started to fill the small space.

"Mia, we're going to get out of here, okay? But I need you to untie the knots from behind my back," he said. Mia looked over at Sage, he was calm and collected as he tried to give her instructions. She knew the only way for her to get out of there would be to listen to him. They were lucky with how they had been tied up because Mia could move her body more freely than Sage could as her hands had been tied in front of her instead of at her back. She did as she was told. As she moved toward Sage, the smoke filled the air and Mia started to cough. She continued to work at the knots and finally managed to free his hands and once his hands were free she brought her hands up to her face as she tried to block out some of the smoke. She watched as Sage worked at the knots around his ankles, loosening them so he could get free.

"Hold on, Mia, we're going to get out of this, I promise,' he said as Mia started to cough a lot more.

Mia was terrified as her breathing started to become a lot more shallow. The smoke in the air filled her lungs and she could feel herself slipping away. She could feel Sage work on her knots, working them until her hands were free.

"Listen to me, Mia, I need you to stay awake for me, okay?" Sage said. Mia tried to open her eyes wider as she started to fade away. She wasn't sure how much longer she could stay awake for. She knew that Sage could get out. He had been trained for worse things in life so she knew that if she couldn't make it at least he would. She didn't want to die but she had started to suffocate as the smoke surrounded them, almost making it hard to see and breathe.

She tried to pick herself up by pushing her arms against the ground but her limbs felt as if they had no strength in them at all. Her arms bent at her elbows as she tried again to push herself off the ground. Internally, Mia started to freak out. She was scared that she was dying. A part of her thought that she could just be weak due to the lack of oxygen.

She felt Sage pick her up and throw her over his shoulder. Her ribs crashed against his shoulder. Mia blacked out as Sage pushed the door open so they could get out of the pantry and out of their burning house.

* * *

ON THE WAY OUT, Sage ran passed a cookie jar. He stopped to open it and was relieved when he felt the gun he had hidden inside of it. He hadn't told Mia about the gun when he had hidden it but he was glad that they didn't keep a lot of sweet snacks in the house or else she would've wanted to use the jar for its proper purpose. He felt like he could fight back because he needed to get Mia outside and into the fresh air. He ran through the house and saw the curtains on fire as well as some of the furniture. His heart broke at the sight of his home, the home he had just gotten used to, the home he had started to build with Mia. He knew he would have to make it up to her. He would stop at nothing to make sure she had everything she wanted. He felt Mia's lifeless body twitch and he started to focus on the task at hand.

As he reached the back door he prepared himself and shifted Mia so he could make sure he could shoot. The moment he pushed himself out, he started to fire. He could barely see it was so dark but he shot in every direction. He tried to fire back into the direction he thought the Omens were, their guns gave their location away so he managed to send a few shots in their direction. His heart was pounding in his chest as he remembered the day in Afghanistan, the day he had also shot into the unknown and hoped for the best. He didn't want to think about that day though. It had been the day he had lost everything and he didn't want to think that way in this situation. He had to believe that they would make it out of there untouched.

He ran toward the woods, ducking as the bullets flew at him. He needed to get to safety, especially because of Mia. He tried to shift her around as he ran so she wouldn't get hit by the flying bullets. He was scared that she would get shot while he ran and he couldn't stand the thought of it.

He ran into the darkness with no light whatsoever but he trusted his instincts as he didn't stop to look back. He already knew there was no saving the house. It was gone and the Omens hadn't caught up to him. He shifted Mia's body so he could cradle her between his arms with her head against his chest. He placed her on the ground and put his head to her chest so he could listen to her heartbeat. He was thankful when he heard it. Even though it was soft, he was still relieved. He looked over her body and realized she hadn't been hit in the crossfire which was great news. At least he knew she hadn't been shot.

"Mia?" he said, as he gently brushed her hair out of her face. "Please wake up," he begged.

Mia didn't move at the sound of his voice and Sage started to get worried. He was alone and didn't know what to do. He wasn't sure if he should do any sort of CPR on Mia considering she was still breathing and he also didn't really know CPR; he hadn't practiced it in years.

Tears started to run down his cheeks as he sat next to Mia's body. He thought he had taken too long. It was possible that Mia could stop breathing altogether and that thought terrified him. He didn't want to believe that she was dying. He couldn't stand to think about it as he sat next to her crying. He hated himself for getting mixed up with the wrong people. Of course, he knew that it was possible that they would've gotten involved with the Omens no matter what they did if they were working with the Screaming Demons but things had just gotten a lot worse than they should've. He thought he should've done more to protect her, he should've tried to get her out of the house quicker or something, anything.

"Mia, you need to wake up. You see I have all these big plans for us. We can get a better house, somewhere closer to the beach and away from city life. We could get out of this mess, we could have whatever you want. I just want you to be happy and alive so I need you to open your eyes, please," Sage said. His voice caught in his throat as his emotions started to pour out of him. He begged her to wake up, he so badly wanted her to open her eyes so he could see her beautiful brown eyes.

He wrapped his hands around one of hers and lifted it to his face as he ran the back of her hand against his cheek. Her body was still warm which he knew was a good sign. He thought she may have just fainted due to the shock and smoke but he couldn't bear looking at her while she was unconscious.

He wasn't ready to say goodbye to Mia and the thought of doing so broke him. He had just gotten over losing Laura and he had finally moved on with the prospect of a new life, a life he thought he'd never get. He didn't want to think negatively but his mind kept going to the worst thoughts he could ever have - Mia dying in front of him. He could still see her chest rising and falling as she continued to breathe gently but he was scared that if he looked away for a second she would stop breathing altogether.

The more he thought about it the worse it got because when he remembered his time in Afghanistan, he had been grateful that he hadn't actually seen his team die. He could remember the bomb going off but after that, most of his memory was blank and as he looked at Mia is was almost too much for him. He would prefer to blackout. He didn't know how much time they had before the Omens would catch up to them but he also didn't want to shake Mia awake in case it scared her. He picked her up and moved further into the woods before placing her back on the ground so she could be comfortable.

16

Mia felt her mind slip away as she became unconscious. She could hear Sage calling for her and she could feel her body move at its own pace but she didn't have any sort of control over what was happening around her. Everything around her was dark and clouded, as if there was an unknown pressure drawing her inside her mind and always from the events that were taking place. She felt as if she were starting to float, and as she got higher and higher she watched from up above what was happening below. It was as if she were having an out-of-body experience before she sank back to the floor.

She could feel a gentle breeze against her face as she lay on the ground. It was fresh and wonderful. She noticed that there was no smoke in the air and her lungs could breathe properly again. She felt herself breathe in deeply and enjoyed the feeling of clean oxygen fill her lungs. She did a few inhales and exhales before she breathed normally.

"You're going to have to open your eyes soon," a voice said from beside her. Mia lay still as she felt the earth beneath her. She stretched her arms out beside her as she ran her fingers through the grass. She was more than happy to just stay on the floor. She couldn't remember the last time she had just closed her eyes and felt the earth beneath her; it must've been years.

"I don't want to open my eyes yet," she whispered. The person laughed at her. Their laugh was soft and gentle, much like her own. It brought her such comfort and peace as she listened to the different tones in their laugh.

"Nothing is going to hurt you if you open your eyes. You're perfectly fine," they said as if to reassure her.

"I know I'm perfectly fine. I can feel all my limbs but I just don't want to wake up yet. It's comfortable here," Mia said. She felt the person gently stroke her face. Their hand was soft and warm.

"You're going to make people believe that you're dead," the person said. Mia didn't care if she looked dead. She hadn't rested that well in a while and she just wanted to prolong it for as long as possible. Everything about her life recently had been so chaotic that she just wanted a moment where nothing was happening. With a sigh, Mia slowly opened her eyes. She wasn't shocked when she saw a different version of herself

sitting next to her. She had recognized her own voice the minute she had spoken.

"What do we do now?" Mia asked herself. The other version of herself sat still for a moment and then in one quick motion she lay down and looked up at the sky. They both lay there in silence and looked at the sky. It was dark and scattered with stars.

"Well, firstly you need to open your eyes in real life and then go from there," she said. She knew she was right.

"Will Sage be there?" she asked. She was scared that she would wake up alone.

"Of course, he's never leaving you," she replied. Deep down she knew she was right. Sage would never leave her and he had made that clear. It was honestly the best feeling she had had in a while; she didn't feel so doomed anymore.

"It's just so relaxing here, it makes it hard to leave," she said. She turned and looked at her other self who was still looking up at the sky.

"I know it is but everything is going to be okay when you open your eyes," she replied.

"Okay, I'll open them in a minute. Let me just enjoy this for a while. It's quiet here and I've missed the quiet," she said as she turned and faced the sky once more.

She watched as the stars twinkled above her. The moon shone brightly and illuminated the trees that were around her.

She felt the ground beneath her conform to the shape of her

body as she melted into it, her body pressed into every inch of the ground beneath her. She felt alive and whole. She knew she didn't have much longer. She could feel the sky slipping away from her as she started to wake up. She wasn't ready to leave yet though, she wanted to stay there and feel the breeze in her hair as she stared at the night sky. It was almost magical. A smile came to her lips as she remembered some of the most magical memories she had. Most of them if not all of them involved Sage. Mia realized that Sage had become the light in her life, pulling her out of the dark and the worst times of her life. She would've died a long time ago if it weren't for him.

"Will I see you again?" she asked herself. She knew in her heart that the version of herself that she was seeing was the stronger version of herself. She was the part of her that knew that she would be okay no matter what and she wished she could take her with her but she also knew that she just needed to believe a little more and then she would be strong.

"Of course, you will," she replied as she reached out and took her hand and as if it was right on cue, Mia could feel herself getting lifted off of the ground and brought back to reality.

Mia could feel her body come back to its full awareness as she felt her mind come back to consciousness. She felt the gentle touch of Sage as he ran his hand against her arm. His touch was soft and made her feel safe. She stayed still for a moment as she savored his touch.

"Mia?" Sage asked from beside her as she slowly opened her eyes. As her surroundings came into focus she could see Sage was looking at her with concern written all over his face and as she looked behind him, she noticed they were no longer in the pantry. It was clear that Sage had stuck to his word about getting them out. She was relieved. He had saved her life and she knew that he would have done anything for her. She knew she must've fainted because of the shock and the smoke but she was a little embarrassed because it had never happened to her before. She had led a pretty faint free life up until then.

"How long have I been out for?" she asked. When she thought back to her dream, she felt as if she had been there for hours. She already missed being in a more dream-like state.

"Only a few minutes, maybe ten max," he replied and as instantly as he replied Mia was swept up into his arms. He wrapped himself around her and held her tightly to his body. She was a little taken aback by the quick movement. "I'm so glad you're awake. I was getting so worried."

She allowed him to hold her for a moment, thankful to be in his arms but as the hug drew out, she felt a little embarrassed and pushed him away from her. She didn't do it to come off as mean but she didn't want him to fuss over her any longer. She still couldn't believe she had fainted. It was a horrifying thought. She had been so useless and helpless at that point and she hated the fact that she wasn't awake to help Sage get out of the house. It must have been a lot of work for him to get them both out of there. She looked him over and noticed that he was fine. He had no marks on his visible skin to show any sort of injury and she was glad.

"I'm sorry you were worried," she whispered as she shifted her body from him. He didn't seem hurt by her sudden change. Instead, he smiled at her. She could see the happiness in his eyes as he stared at her.

"I'm just glad you're awake now. I don't think we should stay here much longer. We need to start finding our way onto the road. There's no way we can go back to the house," he said and she knew he was right.

A part of Mia wouldn't have minded going back to the house just to see the damage that had been caused. It would've killed her to see it but she was curious about how much of her house was left still standing. She had no concept of time so she had no idea how long the fire had been going but she assumed roughly twenty minutes or less. She couldn't remember how long they had been trapped for as it was a bit of a blur to her. She thought about possibly investing in a few gas masks just in case something like this happened again.

It dawned on Mia that they had no way of calling for

help and they had both changed into their pajamas when they had put the movie on so they really weren't prepared to go for a walk in the woods. They didn't have their phones on them so they couldn't even use the built-in flashlights to help see which scared Mia because neither of them had any shoes on. Mia had stayed away from the woods since they had moved there. It had never looked exactly safe and she was scared of what could be lurking in them.

"What do we do now?" Mia asked. She wanted the whole ordeal to be over but she knew it wouldn't end so soon. She turned to face the direction of her house and saw the smoke rising as it filled the air. Her heart sank as she watched the smoke grow bigger as it took over the entire house. She knew everything was gone, everything she had tried to create so it would be a good home to live in was being burnt to the ground.

"We keep going. We need to find someone who can help us," Sage replied. Mia was only half listening as she continued to watch the smoke rise. She could see some of the flames through the trees.

"This is awful," she said. "Why did this have to happen?" she cried as the tears fell down her cheeks. She couldn't hold them in any longer.

"I know it is but at least we're here and not there," he replied as he gently brushed the tears from her face. She was sad and completely heartbroken but Sage was right, at least they had gotten out of the house before either of them was really injured.

"Thank you for saving me," she said.

"There's no need to thank me. There was no way I would have left you behind," he replied.

The love Mia had for Sage grew even more in her heart, and she knew without a doubt that the man that stood before her was the man she wanted to spend the rest of her life with.

"I love you," she said. She knew in her heart that it was as good a time as any to finally say it back to him. He proved to her over and over again that he would do right by her and that was all she ever wanted. Sage stood still beside her, his eyes wide as the words sunk in.

"You don't know how good it is to hear those words come out of your mouth," he replied as he quickly leaned in and kissed her. It was a wonderful moment that broke them away from the negative which helped relax them a bit. It was a truly vulnerable moment. They had both been through so much and lost so much but they had done it together which definitely made them feel closer.

They began to walk through the woods and away from their house. Mia felt as though saying goodbye to their home was like closing a bad chapter of their lives. Of course, it was sad but she felt positive that the worst was over and soon they could start fresh. She knew in her heart that as long as she had Sage by her side, she had no reason to be afraid of anything anymore. Life would never be perfect and she realized that while she was working with the Screaming Demons, it would never be anywhere near perfect but she had found Sage because of them and she didn't regret that.

The woods were dark as they walked. Both of them were a bit nervous about what could be in front of them. They knew that there were snakes, spiders and wild animals in the woods that could come out at any point but they didn't have much of a choice other than continuing to walk forward. Their eyes slowly adjusted to their surroundings until it became a little easier to see around them.

"Do you think it'll get easier from here on out?" Mia asked as they walked. They both stepped carefully as they walked, terrified that they would stand on anything that could potentially injure them. They didn't need to injure themselves after managing to get out of a burning house.

"I honestly don't know. I know for a fact that we'll need to get hold of Fiona as soon as possible so she can hear what's happened but after that, I don't know what will happen," he replied. Sage was right. There was no knowing what would happen next. For all they knew, the Omens could have another attack planned. It was a horrible thought that brought a shiver over Mia. If they had something bigger planned, who knew what it would involve. She was grateful that she didn't have much in Florida that could be destroyed, and she also didn't have any family that the Omens could hold hostage which was definitely good. It was scary to think that if she had been with her family instead of Sage she wouldn't have been able to get out of the house alive. A part of her was happy that she didn't have a close relationship with her family anymore. She would've hated herself for getting them involved in anything that involved the Omens.

The one thing she knew she would always be grateful for was the fact that Sage had been the one she had been trapped with. She imagined if she had been by herself, and the thought didn't sit well with her. She knew she would spend the rest of her life making Sage know how much he meant to her, there wouldn't be a day that would go by where she wouldn't tell him that she loved him.

17

It was silent as they walked forward. The only sound that surrounded them was the sound of their feet as they crushed leaves under their feet. Mia didn't even want to think about how dirty she was. She tried not to think at all as they tried to find the road. It felt as if they had been walking forever in the dark as they heard the sound of animals roaming around them. Mia held on to Sage's hand tightly as they walked and she didn't want to let go.

They continued to walk through the woods and soon they came to the road that connected to the street that led to their house. They knew they couldn't risk being seen so they tried to stay out of view of anyone who drove past. Soon cars started driving past them from their house and they could only imagine that the Omens were finally leaving. Clearly, there wasn't anything left for them to do but leave. A few fire trucks drove past them going toward the house and they waited to see if anyone from the Screaming Demons would show up.

They hoped that even though it was extremely late, someone would have heard about the fire. The Screaming Demons had ways of hearing about these kinds of things. They would both be grateful just to see someone who wasn't an Omen.

It didn't take long for them to notice Adam's truck traveling toward the house in the distance. Sage took the lead and walked out into the road to stop him. He was the only person they could trust. As soon as he came closer he slowly came to a stop and recognized them.

"Oh, thank god you two got out of there. I heard that there's nothing left of it now," Adam said as he got out of his car to greet them. They were so grateful to see him that they almost started crying. They were starting to lose hope that they'd see anyone who could help them. They weren't surprised to hear that there was nothing left of their house. They had said their goodbyes already.

"We're honestly so happy to see you," Sage said as he gave Adam a quick hug. They started to explain what had happened while Adam stood quietly listening. It was a long story and even just retelling it made it all too real for them again.

"Wow. That's so crazy. Well, I'm glad to see you both out of there and alive," Adam said as he gestured them to get into the car. It was time to get out of there, finally.

"Can I use your phone to call Fiona? Mine is probably ashes by now," he said as he turned slightly to the house.

'Of course. It's in the cubbyhole," he said. Sage reached for the phone and dialed Fiona's number. It went straight to voicemail so he left her a message explaining everything. He looked at the time nf the dashboard of the car and noticed it was just after midnight so she was most likely sleeping which of course would be completely understandable.

"Where should we go?" Mia asked. She was sitting near the window looking out as they drove away from the house and away from the fire.

"I think we should go to the club, it's probably the safest place for us to be right now," Sage replied. Adam agreed and drove them to the club.

Once they arrived, Sage and Mia relaxed a bit as they walked into the comfort of the club, their second home. Mia looked around the club and felt all the chairs as she exhaled deeply. She was finding it extremely hard to keep calm. Her emotions were on edge and she was exhausted and ready to pass out.

"Could you imagine if they had burnt this down too?" she asked. She didn't want to think about it but it seemed as though the Omens didn't care about human life at all. Why would they care about burning down another building? Mia could remember hearing them laughing as they had set her house on fire; it was all a game to them.

"I honestly believe I would've killed someone if they had and in all honesty, I feel like killing someone now because of the house," Sage said.

"Don't worry boss, I'll take care of that," Adam said. The thought was scary as Mia heard the tone of Adam's voice. She knew he could be a scary guy if he wanted to be. She didn't want to know what they would do and who would kill whom. All she really wanted to do was sleep. Her body hurt and she just needed rest. Sage felt the same. Even though he wanted to be a part of the hunt for the Omens, he knew he could leave it up to Adam to take care of it.

"I think we need to call some of the guys in," Sage said. He knew that there were 23 Omens that needed to be stopped and as much as he wanted to be the one who ended the lives of the 11 Omens that were at his house, he couldn't go with them. He needed to be with Mia for a while. It had been a hard day for them both. He looked at her with pride as she stood tall after the long day they had had. He was so proud of her for not giving up and just pushing through it.

Sage also knew that he was too emotional to go after the Omens. His temper was high as he thought back. He couldn't be involved in killing them because he would probably enjoy it too much. He wasn't usually the kind of person who found pleasure in someone else's pain but he knew he would love watching the life leave Lorraine's eyes while he killed her. The thought was a bit scary for him which is why he definitely could not go with them. He couldn't become that type of person after everything and especially after all the people he had lost.

Adam started calling some of the guys to help while Sage went over to Mia.

"Maybe we should get a room somewhere for the night?" he asked.

"Yeah, I think that would be a good idea. We don't really have anywhere else to go," Mia replied. Maybe it would be good for them to be completely alone for a while. Sage was sure Mia needed to sleep but possibly also needed to talk. She had been through a lot in the last few hours and he was sure it must be taking a toll on her.

"Oh, you guys don't need to worry about getting a room somewhere, you can sleep at my place," Adam said as he walked closer to them. He had heard some of their conversation between calling some of the guys.

"Oh, that's so kind of you, thank you," Mia said.

Adam passed his keys over to Sage before he continued calling more Screaming Demons.

"We'll just call a cab to get to your place," Sage said. As he said it he wondered if their new car was alright or if they had done something to it before leaving the scene. He couldn't remember it being one of the cars that had driven past them earlier. He was happy he had insured it so even if it wasn't alright they could get something to replace it soon.

"How are you feeling?" Sage asked Mia as they walked out of the club to wait for a cab to collect them. Adam had been nice enough to call a personal one for them considering most taxi companies stopped running at 11 pm.

"I mean emotionally I don't know but physically my body hurts a lot. What about you?" Mia asked. Sage had to think about it for a while. He noticed that his body wasn't actually that sore. His shoulders had started to tense up a little after carrying Mia, not that she was heavy but dead weight wouldn't be easy for anyone to carry. Other than that he felt relatively fine, angry and frustrated but fine.

"I suppose I'm alright, just tired," he replied. He noticed the slump in Mia's shoulders and decided to pull her close to him. He wrapped his arms around her and gently stroked her hair while her head rested against his chest.

The cab pulled up and they made their way to Adam's apartment, grateful that they didn't have to sleep in a hotel for the night.

"What do you think we should do now?" Mia asked as they sat in the back of the car.

"What do you mean?" he asked.

"Well, do you think we should stay with the Screaming Demons or is it time for us to find something else? Like, what if something like this happens again but only much worse?" she asked.

Sage wasn't sure what to say. He'd be lying if he said he hadn't been thinking about their next move but he also didn't think he could leave the Screaming Demons. They had become a family to him and he owed so much to Fiona and Grier that he wasn't sure if he could just walk away from them. He knew they weren't really in the greatest situation but he also couldn't imagine what his life would be like without his job. He knew he could get a new job, maybe something that didn't involve so much messed up shit and the wrong people, but he wasn't sure if it would bring him as much happiness as the life he had created for himself recently.

"Do you think you could walk away from Fiona and Grier? The rest of the Hell Kats?" Sage asked Mia.

"I don't know. I feel as if maybe things would be better if we did walk away but of course, I'd miss everyone. They're family to me too but at the same time, would we be involved in so much bad shit if we walked away?" she asked in return. Sage knew that the chances of them having a more normal and calm life would be slim if they stayed.

"Maybe, maybe not, but where would we be without them?" he asked. He knew he would do whatever he needed to do if it meant Mia was happy. He would cut off his own leg if he had to. It sounded dramatic even as he thought it but he knew it was true; he would do anything for her.

They rode the rest of the cab ride in silence. Both had a lot to think about. Sage didn't know what he would do if he didn't work for the Screaming Demons. Would he go into security or would he do something else altogether? He wasn't sure. If he thought about it he knew he could do anything he put his mind to. He had always been strong-willed when it came to doing things correctly even when he didn't enjoy it.

Once they arrived at Adam's apartment they made their way to the guest room. Both of them were extremely exhausted as they looked at the comfortable bed in front of them. Adam had told them to make themselves at home so they both decided to have a shower before borrowing a few items of clothing. Mia showered first and scrubbed her body clean. Her feet and legs were extremely dirty and her hair smelled of smoke. She felt disgusting as she watched the dirt make its way down the drain. She washed her hair twice just to make sure it was clean before she got out of the shower. She had borrowed an oversized shirt that was long enough to reach mid-thigh and so she put her clothes in the wash before she climbed into bed.

Mia waited for Sage while he went to shower. She was exhausted but couldn't fall asleep as there was too much on her mind. She knew the life she had chosen had been better than the one she almost ended up with but she wasn't sure if she could do it anymore. Sage had almost died when he had been kidnapped and then they had both almost died when their house had been set on fire. She hated to think what might happen next. She knew they could only beat death so many times that before it caught up with them and she didn't want to think that being involved with the Screaming Demons would cause that to finally happen. She loved them, she loved the Hell Kats, she loved the Screaming Demons and she really loved Fiona. She had learned so much since being a part of their world and their team but at what cost? If she thought about having any sort of normal life she couldn't picture herself still working with the Screaming Demons. It was the only way she saw it.

Sage joined her in the bedroom a few minutes after

he had finished his shower. They were both extremely happy to be clean and in clean clothes.

"Are you hungry? I'm sure Adam wouldn't mind if we make something to eat, " Sage said. Although they hadn't eaten much the day before, neither of them were that hungry.

"I'm okay, I'll just wait for breakfast. It's 1 am already," she replied. Mia's body melted into the bed as she relaxed further into the mattress Sage soon joined her and they cuddled up close to each other.

"You know, I keep thinking about what our life would be like without all of this and yet something keeps telling me that I wouldn't have you if I didn't have all of this. I mean, we may not have even met if it weren't for Fiona and the Screaming Demons," Mia said as she rested her head against his chest. They both knew she was right. It was doubtful that their lives would have crossed paths if they didn't know the Screaming Demons. Sage could've gotten a job somewhere else and Mia would have either been still involved with the Omens or possibly dead. Mia didn't want to think about her near-death experiences; she was grateful to be alive.

She moved closer to Sage, as close as she could possibly get as she felt the warmth of his body against hers. She had been so close to never feeling it again and as she lay there she inhaled deeply and relaxed completely after the day they had had. Sage was also extremely happy to be close to Mia, feeling her skin next to his sent a feeling of love through his body like never before. They fell asleep in each other's arms and they both dreamt of a life where they were happy and healthy.

18

Mia woke up a few times throughout the early hours of the morning, scared that someone was in the house to finish the job. When she woke up, she just laid still for a while and listened to her surroundings. When she heard a creek or any sort of noise, her heart raced. She knew a part of her was being irrational but she couldn't help herself. She was unsure as to whether or not the Omens would find them, or if the Screaming Demons had already taken care of them. The thought of the Screaming Demons killing or 'taking care' of the Omens scared her a little. She knew it would be violent and dangerous especially considering they had crossed a line. Sage and Mia were the leaders in Florida and she knew that the Screaming Demons would look after them at all times. She was grateful she didn't have to be a part of the aftermath; she didn't want to think about it.

She thought about her life as if it were normal and she could picture herself painting as her career. It was a good image in her mind as she saw herself painting landscapes and people. Her mind went back to the paintings she had lost in the fire and her heart broke a little. There had been so many paintings that had been done when she had needed to release her emotions and there were beautiful ones of Sage too which were all gone. She looked over at the man she loved so much as he slept and she knew that she could paint better pictures of him going forward because now the love she had for him had been reciprocated.

Mia tried to convince herself that she would be fine if she went to sleep. She told herself over and over again that there would be no need to worry about anyone breaking into Adam's house. As she struggled to sleep, she decided to get up and walk around Adam's house, just to see how he lived. She was pleasantly surprised to see that he kept his house really clean and well-stocked. The way he had decorated was also really nice and she took in a few ideas for when she got to decorate her new house. She supposed she was excited to see where they would live.

She went back to the bedroom and cuddled up against Sage once more and listened to his breathing. It was the perfect sound for her as she closed her eyes to sleep.

She tossed and turned as she tried to fall back to sleep. It took a few minutes but eventually, her eyes closed as her breathing got heavier and soon she slipped into unconsciousness.

Mia was sitting on the beach and the salty breeze was flowing around her, making her hair blow in every direction. She closed her eyes and allowed herself to fully enjoy the feeling. She felt free and calm as if there was nothing else in the world that could bother her. She rested her hands beside her, sinking them into the sand around her. She let the sand seep through her fingers as she picked up handfuls and separated her fingers so the sand could run through them. It was tranquil and quiet as she listened to the wind as it whipped around her. She could hear birds in the distance and envied their ability to fly. She longed to be up and over the sea.

"It's so beautiful, isn't it?" someone asked. She opened her eyes to turn and came face to face with Sage as he sat down next to her. She smiled as the sun hit his face, setting his eyes on fire as they hypnotized her. He looked as if he had expected to see her there.

"It really is," she said in agreement. She turned back to the ocean and watched as the sun had started to set. The waves transformed from a gentle blue to all sorts of pinks, yellows, oranges, and reds. It was breathtaking. She knew she could

watch the sunset over and over again and it would never be enough for her.

"This is one of my favorite places," Sage said as he watched the sunset. Mia already knew why it was his favorite place, they had been there before. They both slipped into a better state of mind as the memory came back to them.

"This will always be one of my favorite places," Mia said. She looked over at Sage and couldn't believe she had been lucky enough to have found him. She knew that her life would never be the same without him. He had already brought so much joy and happiness into her life that she didn't want to picture her life without him. She reached her hand out and intertwined her fingers with his. Gently she leaned against his shoulder as they continued to watch the sunset.

"We could stay like this forever and I'd be happy," Sage said as he squeezed her hand slightly. She agreed. It was magical being there with him. She felt a sense of forever like they were going to be together forever and her heart soared at the thought.

"Me too," she replied. Deep down she knew that wherever they were, she'd be happy as long as he was with her.

She closed her eyes and took in the feeling of contentment and love as the sun vanished.

Mia woke up in the morning and stretched her body out next to Sage. He was still sleeping as she wiggled her toes and brought her hands up above her head, allowing her body to release all the tension she had been carrying since the day before. She felt a lot better knowing that it was a new day. Of course, she knew that there were a lot of things that needed to be sorted out but she didn't feel like there was any rush. Her life wasn't in danger at that moment and she didn't feel as if she needed to get out of bed yet.

She decided to bury herself in the bed, covering herself with the blanket so she could relax a little more. She didn't think anyone would complain if she stayed in bed the whole day. She assumed most people would understand considering what she had been through so she closed her eyes and fell back to sleep.

After sleeping for another thirty minutes her body woke her up again and she knew it was time to get the day started. She wasn't the type of person who would let daylight slip away without enjoying it.

She leaned over and gently kissed Sage's cheek while he slept. A gentle snore escaped his lips. She wondered what he could be dreaming about as a smile crossed his lips. He looked extremely peaceful and comfortable as he reached out and wrapped his arms around her. Soon enough she was tucked into his arms with his head resting on hers.

"Good morning," he whispered sleepily. He inhaled and exhaled deeply.

"Good morning to you too," she replied with a smile. She would never get tired of waking up next to Sage, especially since he always looked so cute in the morning.

"How did you sleep?" he asked. Mia's mind remembered the dream she had had and it brought a smile to her face once more.

"I slept very well, and yourself?" she asked in return. Sage lay silent for a moment.

"Yes, I slept very well too," he said with a huge grin. Mia wondered if he had had a dream as good as hers. She also wondered if he dreamt of her as often as she dreamt of him and at that thought, a blush covered her cheeks.

"You're so beautiful in the morning," he said as he traced circles on her exposed skin. She was in heaven. Her stomach growled against her will and she realized that she was starving.

"I suppose now is a good time to have breakfast," Sage said with a laugh as he heard the noise.

"I think that would be a good idea," she replied. Her body felt a little weak as she stood up. She gave herself a moment just so she could stretch again while she stood. Her feet ached from all the walking she had done during the night but she was very happy that she hadn't stepped in anything that could've injured her. Her muscles were tight as she stretched and her head was a little foggy from the smoke.

"How does your body feel?" she asked Sage. When

she looked over at him, he was also doing a few stretches.

"A little sore but could be much worse," he replied. Mia was happy that he always seemed to look on the bright side of things especially when she couldn't. It definitely helped make her days a lot brighter.

"I think we should look into getting a massage soon. I'd say we deserve a treat," she said. She laughed and then smiled.

"I definitely agree with you there," he replied. She thought about being the one to give Sage a massage and she got all flustered. She knew it wasn't the time to be thinking of such things but as she watched him stretch, revealing some flesh, all she wanted to do was reach out and touch him.

Mia wasn't sure if Adam was back yet or if he was awake and she didn't know if she wanted him to see her in one of his shirts so she quickly went to fetch her clean clothes before she left the room and headed for the kitchen.

When she reached the kitchen she was happy she had decided to change because Adam was awake and sitting in the kitchen. He looked extremely tired as Mia noticed the bags under his eyes but he smiled at her when he saw her.

"Morning," he said. Mia wondered when he had gotten home.

"Good morning, you look exhausted," she said as she walked over to the kettle so she could make herself a cup of coffee.

"It was definitely a process this morning but it's done," he replied and when he smiled Mia noticed it reached his eyes and they looked slightly devilish.

"What do you mean?" she asked.

"The Omens, they won't be a problem anymore," he said. He winked at her then and she got a feeling in her stomach that he meant that the Omens had been 'taken care' of. She didn't want to ask too many questions but she was still curious.

"Why won't they be a problem anymore?" she asked. Adam shifted in his seat. She could tell that he was thinking about whether or not he should tell her more.

"You don't need to worry about that," he replied, clearly deciding not to give her any information. She knew that if she were to hear what had happened she might be sick. It could've only gone one way, especially if they weren't going to be a problem anymore.

She wasn't sure how she felt about the situation. She knew the Omens were a threat, they had been a threat to the Screaming Demons long before she had even arrived in the picture but it had been the life of the Screaming Demons to have enemies. It had been that way from the very beginning. A part of her thought about the 23 Omens who weren't going to be a problem anymore and she wondered how their lives had ended. Had it been horrible? The thought made bile travel up into her mouth. She swallowed hard against the urge to vomit as she focused on making her coffee and took out a mug for Sage too.

Sage walked into the kitchen then and joined Mia at the kettle.

He looked over at Adam. "How's it going?" he asked as he took the cup of coffee Mia offered him.

"Great man, just great. Today is the start of something new for all of us," he replied. Mia knew what he meant. It was the day they no longer had to worry about having any enemies. Sage seemed to know exactly what Adam was saying as he slapped him on the back before they hugged. Mia didn't know how she felt about the whole thing. She knew she should be happy and grateful that they didn't have to worry anymore but she couldn't help but feel as if the whole thing could've been avoided from the very beginning.

She didn't say anything about how she felt as she knew they wouldn't understand.

"Alright, gents, since we're celebrating things, shall we celebrate with a good breakfast?" she asked. She wanted to change the topic and the only thing she really wanted was breakfast. She was so hungry she could have eaten a whole chicken.

"Breakfast sounds like a great idea," Adam said. She

looked around the kitchen for a bit and decided to make omelets for them. It would take her a while to prepare each one and she liked the idea of keeping herself busy. She knew nothing would be the same going forward and she wasn't sure what to expect. Of course, she knew that Sage didn't want to leave the Screaming Demons and really neither did she but she hoped that they wouldn't have to be involved in anything so crazy ever again. She didn't want any more gunfights and gangs of people showing up unannounced at her house threatening her life. She could honestly do without all the drama so she hoped there could be a way to make that happen.

She knew it had all made her a stronger person. Everything they had gone through from her then Sage being kidnapped and to them almost dying. Her life had been crazy and fun all at the same time which she knew was a good thing. Most people led boring lives and although she wished her life wasn't as crazy as it was, she knew that she would always come out on top. She was nowhere near the same person she was when she had first joined the Screaming Demons and she was happy to see just how strong she could be.

Mia looked over at Sage as he talked with Adam. She could see how happy he was with the news and she didn't blame him. Out of the two of them, he had had a lot worse done to him than what had happened the night before. It made her happy to see him being so carefree as she watched him laugh and joke. It was a sight she hadn't seen in a while. She really wasn't sure what would happen once Fiona and Grier heard the news but their lives seemed to be looking up. Hopefully, everything would turn around for the better going forward.

19

few months had gone by and things between Sage and Mia were better than ever. They had managed to find a new house, one that was close to the beach so they could watch the sunset every day. It was the one time of the day they would always make available for each other, no matter what. It had made them closer as the days passed and they were both extremely happy about it. Their relationship had taken all sorts of hits and they seemed to come out stronger every time.

Sage had learned that Mia was possibly the strongest woman he had ever met and to him, that was one of her greatest features. He learned that she could be strong no matter what and he loved that about her. He knew it had been extremely hard on her when the fire happened, especially when they lost their home but she showed how strong she was when they went looking for something new. She didn't complain much about their loss but took it in her stride.

Everything had gone back to normal. The business was rebuilt but excluding the drugs. Fiona and Grier agreed that it would be better for everyone if they just focused on running a clean business. No one wanted to get caught up with any other bad people who could potentially ruin their lives. It had been too much already for all of them. Fiona and Grier came to Florida soon after the fire and had promised to make things better for the future. Everyone could see that the relationship between Sage and Mia was different which Fiona was happy about. Of course, she had seen the connection between the two of them before they had and she was glad they had finally gotten together. It would make the business work better because they were stronger than ever.

Everyone celebrated the fact that the Omens wouldn't be around anymore. It was a great time for the Screaming Demons. When the Omens had been involved, they always had to worry about things going wrong. They all knew it had to do with their line of work as well, but they had been doing it for so long that there was no point in changing that until it became too dangerous.

Sage knew that it was the right time for him to settle down. He had realized through everything that Mia was the one for him. It was a scary thought to have after all the pain he had gone through previously but he knew he could trust her. He trusted her with his life and he would trust her with his heart. It had taken him so long to finally admit to himself how he truly felt about her and he had to make sure she understood that he was in it until the very end. He wanted to grow old with Mia, raise children with her and then die by her side. He could not picture his life without her in it and that was something he had never thought would happen.

He had watched Mia build a new life for them after their house had been burnt down and he could see how hard she tried to make it the best home possible. He loved the fact that she had chosen a place that was near the beach; he knew the significance. It meant the world to him that she hadn't given up on their relationship when he had spoken to her about staying with the Screaming Demons. She had been so understanding about his needs that he loved her even more.

He knew the next step for them was to get married. He wanted to do everything the right way when it came to Mia, he wanted to give her the life she deserved. She had never spoken to him about marriage and he knew it was because she was too scared to bring up the topic due to his past but he could picture himself with her forever so there was no point in prolonging it. He was grateful that she had been so patient with him. He knew it must've been hard and sometimes he couldn't understand why she had stuck around for so long when there had never been a proper talk about the future.

It was a bright and sunny afternoon when he decided to go look for a ring that suited Mia and her personality; he wanted it to be perfect. It wasn't just about the moment but he wanted to prove to her that he knew her inside out. Getting the right ring just meant that the whole moment would be perfect.

"I'm just going out for a while, maybe we can meet up later at the bar?" Sage asked Mia while she sat on the patio that looked out onto the beach. She looked at peace as she watched the waves hit the shore. It was beautiful. Sage loved the fact that they lived so close to the beach because the smell of the ocean helped calm him a bit.

"Okay, that sounds like an idea. I'll meet you there in a few hours?" she asked.

"That sounds great, I'll see you there," Sage replied. He knew she had no idea what he had planned for them later. He had kept his feelings about marriage to himself.

He left her at the house and made his way to a jewelry store that he had heard of. He had a picture in his mind of what kind of ring he wanted for Mia. He knew it had to be simple and he had researched pictures online so he would have an idea of what to look for. He decided that he liked the idea of a Princess cut, with a 1-

carat stone set in a silver band. It was just elegant enough but also not too over the top since Mia didn't wear jewelry.

Once he arrived at the store, he made his way over to the assistant behind the counter.

"Good day, sir. How may I help you?" he asked.

"Hi, I'm looking for something like this," Sage said as he pulled out his phone to show him the picture he had on his phone.

"Oh, an excellent choice. Follow me," he replied as he walked Sage over to a counter that had a glass case to display the ring selection. He glanced over the rings and within an instant saw the ring he wanted.

"I'll take that one, please," he said. It was very similar to the picture he had on his phone and he knew it was the right one. He didn't really worry about the price of it, he never really worried about money while working for Fiona and Grier.

"Perfect, sir. Let me cash it up and you can be on your way," the assistant said.

Sage watched as the assistant placed the ring in a very beautiful maroon box and tied it up with a ribbon. He paid and left the store.

He spent a bit of time walking around the shops before he made his way to the bar. He wanted to rehearse what he was going to say because he wanted to make sure it was perfect. There was a part of him that wished they were in Pine Hill for the proposal. He felt that because they had met in the bar there it would've been the perfect place to propose as if it were a complete circle of their relationship. He didn't mind so much that he couldn't do it there though. He just wanted the moment to be perfect. He hadn't planned anything really special but he had invited Fiona and Grier to join for drinks so they could be there. After all, it was thanks to Fiona that Sage had been put with Mia in the first place.

He made his way to the club and decided to stop for some flowers on his way, just so he wasn't completely empty-handed. When he got to the club, he walked straight over to the bar to order a drink.

"Hey, Adam. Please can I get-" he started.

"A whiskey on the rocks?" Adam finished. He already knew exactly what Sage drank.

"You know me too well," Sage said with a laugh. Adam and Sage had gotten much closer after the fire. They both knew the importance of getting rid of the Omens and they had bonded over it making their friendship bloom.

"Of course. So how are you feeling?" Adam asked. Sage had told him about his plan to propose to Mia. He was the only person who actually knew it was going to happen.

"You know, I'm not feeling too bad. A little nervous but other than that rather confident that she'll say yes," he replied. He wasn't 100 percent sure that she would say yes but he hoped that he had read the signs correctly. He knew Mia loved him and he felt as if she was ready to take their relationship to the next level.

He had noticed a change in her behavior and it seemed that she was ready for more. She hadn't said it in words but he hoped he had picked up the right signals. It wasn't that she spoke about marriage around him but she seemed to be into the very romantic side of things, cooking them wonderful meals in candlelight that just seemed to be oddly romantic for their usual dinners. He thought she was ready since they had already been through so much together and they had gotten tattoos to symbolize their relationship before they had even said the words 'I love you' to each other.

He sat at the bar and waited for her to arrive. His nerves grew as the time ticked by. They hadn't discussed a time so she could show up at any point. After what felt like years of waiting, Mia showed up at the bar. Sage watched as she walked over to him with a huge smile on her face. She was wearing a light summer dress that was loose and flowy. It was printed with different colored flowers and her skin glowed.

God, she's beautiful, he thought to himself.

"Hey you," she said as she took a seat next to him. He leaned over and kissed her cheek.

"Hey to you too. You look stunning," he said.

"Oh, stop it. You're going to make me blush," she said shyly. A blush had already started to cross her face.

"I see it's a bit too late to stop that from happening," he teased. She gently pushed him on his stool and he tried not to fall off.

"Hush before I slap you," she joked.

"What would you like to drink?" he asked with a bit of a laugh. He would've ordered something for her but she often changed her drink choices.

"I'll have a glass of white wine, please," she said. Adam was close by so Sage didn't need to repeat her drink order. Sage sat nervously next to Mia as she took a sip of her wine. He wasn't sure how he would start the process of asking Mia to marry him but he knew he needed to do it soon before he chickened out.

"So how has your day been so far?" he asked.

"It's been good, and yours?" she replied.

"It's been great, thank you. But there is something I need to ask you which could make it that much better," Sage said.

"Oh, really. And what's that?" Mia asked. She looked at him with eyes filled with curiosity.

"Well, you see the thing is, you've changed my life, Mia. When I met you I was a very broken man, possibly at the lowest possible point of my life. I didn't have much hope for having a life I actually enjoyed. I had cut myself off from feeling anything toward anyone and then in you entered and everything changed. You were a sudden burst of light in all my dark days and you fought for me like no one has before. There is no way in hell I ever want to live my life without you by my side," Sage said. Everyone in the club had stopped while the music had been turned down so they could all listen. Fiona and Grier had just entered as Sage had started his speech so they stood silently near the entrance of the club and waited.

Mia sat still on her stool, taking in what Sage was saying with wide eyes. He could tell she knew where the conversation was going. He wasn't sure how he should take her reaction as she didn't make any move to stop him. He had been scared she would leave halfway through.

"Sage…" she said. She was completely speechless as he raised a hand to gently quiet her.

"I'm not done yet… It's taken me a long time to get over my past and you know that. You have always been so understanding and so patient with me that I knew if I didn't make you mine forever, I'd be the stupidest man on this planet. So, Mia Giovanni, would you please make me the luckiest man in the world and marry me?" he finally asked. "We could have a small, simple wedding on the beach, but all I ask is that you marry me."

He slid off of his stool and proceeded to go down on one knee. Slowly he pulled out the box from his back pocket and tugged at the ribbon so he could open it to reveal the ring that laid inside. Mia drew in a deep breath as she looked at the ring that shone brightly in the club lights.

No one said a word as Sage waited for Mia to reply.

* * *

MIA STOOD shell-shocked in front of Sage and everyone else in the club. She knew she loved Sage and she would love him until she died but she hadn't thought about marriage. She wasn't sure she was the marrying type. She had never thought about it properly before. She supposed it had something to do with the fact that she had never loved anyone so much before either. She looked at everyone who had started to watch the proposal unfold and she didn't know what to say. She knew she wanted Sage, she had wanted him the moment she met him, but marrying him was something so much bigger. She could remember the dreams she had had in the past about having children with him and getting married. She did like the idea but she had not expected it to happen at that moment. Sage looked at her longingly, waiting for her to say something and he hoped she wouldn't say no. The suspense of it all hung heavily in the air.

20

One month later, Sage and Mia were cuddled in bed, loving every minute they got to spend with each other as two separate people because it wouldn't be long until that changed.

All her life, Mia longed for someone to love her properly. Of course, her parents had loved her to a certain extent but she wanted a partner who loved her for who she was and that partner was Sage. She knew he would love her no matter what and she trusted that he would do right by her every single day. He was a dream come true for her and she hoped she was for him too.

Mia knew that her life had changed forever when she met Sage. She knew that she could never picture herself with anyone but him and she had just waited for him to catch up with how she felt. She had been patient with him because she didn't want to lose him and she thanked her lucky stars that he had allowed himself to open up to her and actually feel his true feelings. She had known in her heart for the longest time that she wanted to be with him for the rest of her life.

She remembered the first time she had seen him at the club and how she was drawn to him instantly as if he were a lighthouse that was bringing her back safely to the life she should have. She never dreamed that it would be filled with so much drama and so many ups and downs but she wouldn't have changed it for the world. Her life had been dull and almost lifeless when she had met Sage and she was happy that she had met him so her life could've turned around for the better. She knew there was no way she could ever thank him for the role he played in her life but she wanted to spend the rest of her life trying. It didn't matter to her where in the world they would be going forward. All she knew was the fact that she wanted to be with Sage wherever he was.

She thought about how he made her feel as she stood outside city hall, her hand tightly wrapped up in Sage's hand. He had made her fall in love with herself and that was more than she had ever thought would happen. It wasn't that she hated herself as much as she just didn't like the life she had. She knew what laid before them would change everything and she was so ready for it.

Her heart sped in her chest as they walked through the doors.

Mia sat in silence for a moment as she thought through her answer. It would be the choice that would change her life forever. She knew without a doubt that she wanted to be with Sage and although she made him wait painfully, she already knew her answer. It was obvious that she would marry him, she would grow old with him and have a happy life with him. She had wanted that from the very beginning. It seemed like such an easy choice to make as she looked into his eyes which begged for an answer. She knew he must be going crazy, thinking he had done the wrong thing when he had done the right thing. Mia knew it had taken everything inside of him to let his guard down and the fact that he wanted to marry her meant more to than he'd ever be able to understand.

"Sage, you crazy, beautiful man, you are out of your mind if you think I wouldn't spend the rest of my life with you," she said as she placed her hands on either side of his face before crushing her lips against his. He pushed himself up off of the ground as he wrapped his arms around her waist, kissing her with everything he had. They kissed passionately as the room exploded into screams of joy. Everyone was extremely happy with the outcome. The air that had felt tight and tense broke out with joy as everyone cheered them on. Everyone knew that they were supposed to be together. They had watched as their relationship had grown into love. It was a magical moment as Sage slipped the ring onto Mia's hand. He was happy that it

fitted her without any problems. Her lips broke out into a huge smile as he pulled her back into him for another kiss. They were both so over the moon at their engagement that they almost forgot that there were people around as they kissed.

Mia had decided that she didn't want a huge wedding. Neither of them had many family members they could invite and they really didn't want to cater to everyone from the club. They both knew that it would've been an expensive wedding and although having a beach wedding sounded nice since the beach was their favorite place, Mia didn't want to make too much of a fuss about it. The most important thing to her was the fact that she was marrying Sage. To her, nothing else mattered. She didn't care about what they looked like or what they were wearing, she just wanted to seal the deal with the man she loved. When they had discussed options, Mia thought it would be just perfect if they went to city hall and signed the papers on their own before heading to the club to celebrate. No one fought her on it when she had mentioned it to people. They were all just happy that they could be involved in the end.

The day was as beautiful as ever. Everything just screamed happy as the sun shone high in the sky while no clouds covered the bright blue skies.

Mia and Sage made their way to the club, holding

each other's hand tightly in the back of the cab. She looked down at her hand and smiled when she saw the rings, one was her engagement ring and the other was her wedding ring. She loved her engagement ring. It truly showed the type of person she was and she was happy that Sage knew her well enough not to have bought her a huge ring.

Her heart soared as they sat in the back of the cab giggling and kissing. It was hard to believe that their lives had reached a moment of pure bliss after everything that had happened. It seemed almost unreal to them as the realization of it all sunk in.

"Can you believe that we got this lucky?" Sage asked as if reading her mind. He smiled at her while his body glowed. He was a sight for sore eyes.

"I didn't think so, but look at us," she replied with a smile as she lifted their hands and pointed to their wedding bands. Sage smiled and lifted their hands to his lips so he could kiss her wedding ring.

"Do you think everyone will be there?" he asked. He already knew no one would miss the chance of seeing them at that moment.

"I believe so. This is going to be a very fun reception," she said.

"I'm really excited but not as excited as I am to be spending the rest of my life with you," Sage said. They glowed as the love they shared surrounded them and created a little bubble that no one could pop.

"You think you're the lucky one? I got to fall in love with you when I least expected to," she said as she kissed him gently. Her life seemed complete at the thought of having Sage with her. Against all odds, they had made it through everything that had been thrown their way.

"I want to be soppy with you but you're going to make me cry," he teased. Mia loved how cute Sage could be when he let himself enjoy a moment for what it truly was. She knew he over-thought a lot of things and she was happy to see him open himself up more.

Sage had never felt so much love for a person his entire life. Falling for Mia had been something so new and easy that he couldn't believe he hadn't seen it sooner. He would think back to when he had tried to push her away and he was extremely grateful that she had stuck around instead of walking away from his bull-shit. She was the strongest person he knew and he couldn't wait to make her feel safe and protected going forward. It helped that the Screaming Demons no longer worked with drugs. The business would stay clean as long as Sage was in control. He couldn't risk putting Mia's life in danger ever again.

When they finally arrived at the club, they stood outside together for a while, kissing and holding each other for a moment before greeting everyone that waited for them inside.

"Are you ready?" he asked. Mia looked beautiful in a simple white dress while Sage had bought a suit for the day. He wanted to take a mental picture of the woman he had married. She was more than he had ever hoped for.

"I'm ready," she replied as she took his hand and pulled him toward the doors. They could hear very loud music coming from inside the club; the party had begun without them. They kissed one last time before walking through the doors.

They were welcomed by all the Screaming Demons and Hell Kats as well as Fiona and Grier. Confetti filled the air as they made their way through the crowd of people who were happy to see them. Everyone had dressed up semi-formally to join in on the special occasion. Mia and Sage couldn't stop smiling as they saw their family, the family they had been welcomed into with open arms and the family that meant so much to them. It was hard to believe that not so long ago they didn't know the people around them, they wouldn't have been able to name any of them. It was amazing that they had met so many wonderful people.

"Hey, guys, you're basically glowing," Adam said as they made their way to the bar.

"Oh, hush," Mia replied as she blushed.

Fiona and Grier made their way over to them and hugged them both.

"We're so happy for you two," Fiona said with tears in her eyes. Sage and Mia loved Fiona so much for everything she had done for them. They knew there would be no way for them to thank her enough.

"You know, Fiona, we have you to thank for this and honestly as much as I didn't like the fact that you pushed us together when we got here, I know now that it was meant to be. I knew then that you knew what you were doing and because I was so blind I couldn't see the bigger picture but this woman is my wife because of you," Sage said. The tears in Fiona's eyes slid down her cheeks at a much faster rate as Sage said his little speech.

"Well, you're very welcome," she muttered as she wiped her tears away. They said a few more words before both couples turned to the dance floor to watch the crowd around them.

The atmosphere in the club was amazing. Everyone was dancing and having a great time which brought them all closer together. It was a happy moment for everyone.

"Shall we dance?" Sage asked Mia who had begun to sway with the music.

"Oh, yes, we shall," she replied as she grabbed his hand and led him to the dance floor. The music was upbeat and soon they both moved to the beat, laughing and smiling at each other as they enjoyed the party. It was a moment neither of them would forget.

Their lives had connected so unexpectedly and yet it was right. If anything they both believed that they had been drawn together because it was meant to be. Neither of them had believed in soul mates until they had met each other but they knew without a doubt that they were soul mates. It wasn't just about looks as much as it was about how they made each other feel. They were lucky enough to have found each other.

The music changed into something softer. It was a song they could slow dance to. Everyone left the dance floor and created a circle around them as Sage took Mia into his arms and danced with her for the first time as husband and wife. She rested her head against his shoulder as they spun around the dance floor. Their bodies came together as if they were one. There was no space between them as they savored the feeling of their first dance.

"I love you, Mia," Sage said as he held her body close to his. Mia lifted her head and looked him in the eyes. They both had love and tears in their eyes, tears of joy.

"I love you too, Sage," she replied. They kissed passionately for a moment while everyone made a noise. Sage pulled Mia off the dance floor and went to the office. He wanted to be with her privately.

"Do you remember the first time we were in here?" he asked as he closed and locked the door behind them.

"How could I forget?" she replied with a wink.

Sage made his way over to Mia and placed a hand on either side of her face before taking her mouth with his. He pressed himself against her as she wrapped her arms around his neck. Both of them wanted and needed each other. Mia moaned as the kiss deepened. In no time, their mouths were open so their tongues could connect. Mia reached for Sage's shirt and pulled it free from his pants so she could touch his skin. It was hot and heavy as Sage moved his hands to the straps of her dress and tugged them off of her shoulders. He leaned forward and kissed each one, feeling the love he had for her in every touch. They touched and felt every inch of each other as they kissed and exposed more skin. Sage's shirt found its way to the floor as Mia undid the buttons and removed it from his body, while Sage slipped Mia's dress down her body until it pooled at her feet. There was no stopping them as Sage took Mia for himself, owning her body as he removed her underwear along with his so he could have her. Their bodies moved together as he went inside her. Their moaning matched as they synced into one, and just as if they were completely connected they fell apart together in a pile of sweat and love.

TWISTED INTENTION
~ A billionaire revenge romance series ~
Twisted Beauty
Twisted Love
Twisted Fate

Mafia's Obsession
~ A hot mafia romance series ~
Mafia's Dirty Secret
Mafia's Fake Bride
Mafia's Final Play

Screaming Demons
~ An MC romance series full of suspense ~
Rough Start
Rough Ride
Rough Choice
Rough Patch
Rough Return
Rough Road
Rough Trip
Rough Night
Rough Love

Standalone Contemporary Romance
Billionaire in Vegas
Billionaire Hunt

Billionaire's Game
Billionaire Retreat
Billionaire On Air
A Chance To Love
Somebody To Love
Not Mine To Love

Check out Summer's entire collection at
www.summercooper.com/books

ABOUT SUMMER COOPER

Thank you so much for reading. Without you, it wouldn't be possible for me to be a full-time author. I hope you enjoy reading my books as much as I do writing them.

Besides (obviously!) reading and writing, I also love cuddling my dogs, shouting at Alexa, being upside down (aka Yoga) and driving my family cray-cray!

Get in touch at
hello@summercooper.com
www.summercooper.com

facebook.com/summercooperauthor
instagram.com/summercooperauthor
goodreads.com/summercooper
bookbub.com/profile/summer-cooper

www.ingramcontent.com/pod-product-compliance
Lightning Source LLC
Chambersburg PA
CBHW031237210726
48287CB00003B/804